Aidan leaned
forward to try to capture Penelope's
gaze.

She smiled, but there was no happiness there. "Sure. Why wouldn't it be?"

"It's just that you got awfully quiet there for a moment."

"I was just thinking...."

What? What had she been thinking? Aidan refused to speak the question aloud, but he found he was curious about Penelope in a way he hadn't been curious about a woman in a long time. He was filled with a desire to reach out and touch her, to urge out whatever it was she was holding in her mind...in her heart.

He found himself reaching out to cup her chin. Just a gentle play of his fingertips up along the delicate line of her jaw. So soft. He wanted to assure her that everything would be okay.

She blinked those big dark eyes, appearing startled yet curious as her tongue darted out to moisten her lips.

Lips Aidan wanted more than anything to kiss. And in the next instant, he w

Dear Reader,

Well, if it's true that March comes in like a lion and goes out like a lamb, you're going to need some fabulous romantic reads to get you through the remaining cold winter nights. Might we suggest starting with a new miniseries by bestselling author Sherryl Woods? In *Isn't It Rich?*, the first of three books in Ms. Wood's new MILLION DOLLAR DESTINIES series, we meet Richard Carlton, one of three brothers given untold wealth from his aunt Destiny. But in pushing him toward beautiful—if klutzy—PR executive Melanie Hart, Aunt Destiny provides him with riches that even money can't buy!

In *Bluegrass Baby* by Judy Duarte, the next installment in our MERLYN COUNTY MIDWIVES miniseries, a handsome but commitment-shy pediatrician shares a night of passion with a down-to-earth midwife. But what will he do when he learns there might be a baby on the way? Karen Rose Smith continues the LOGAN'S LEGACY miniseries with *Take a Chance on Me*, in which a sexy, single CEO finds the twin sister he never knew he had—and in the process is reunited with the only woman he ever loved. In *Where You Least Expect It* by Tori Carrington, a fugitive accused of a crime he didn't commit decides to put down roots and dare to dream of the love, life and family he thought he'd never have. Arlene James wraps up her miniseries THE RICHEST GALS IN TEXAS with *Tycoon Meets Texan!* in which a handsome billionaire who can have any woman he wants sets his sights on a beautiful Texas heiress. She clearly doesn't need his money, so *whatever* can she want with him? And when a police officer opens his door to a nine-months-pregnant stranger in the middle of a blizzard, he finds himself called on to provide both personal and professional services, in *Detective Daddy* by Jane Toombs.

So bundle up, and take heart—spring is coming! And so are six more sensational stories about love, life and family, coming next month from Silhouette Special Edition!

All the best,

Gail Chasan
Senior Editor

Please address questions and book requests to:
Silhouette Reader Service
U.S.: 3010 Walden Ave., P.O. Box 1325, Buffalo, NY 14269
Canadian: P.O. Box 609, Fort Erie, Ont. L2A 5X3

Where You Least Expect It

TORI CARRINGTON

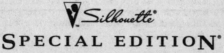

Silhouette

SPECIAL EDITION

Published by Silhouette Books

America's Publisher of Contemporary Romance

We warmly dedicate this book
to Terri and Mike Medeiros, Brenda and Jim Chin,
Leslie and Bruce Kelly, Christine and Richard Feehan
and couples everywhere who have found love
where they least expected it. You inspire us....

 SILHOUETTE BOOKS

ISBN 0-373-24600-5

WHERE YOU LEAST EXPECT IT

Copyright © 2004 by Lori and Tony Karayianni

Visit Silhouette at www.eHarlequin.com

Printed in U.S.A.

Books by Tori Carrington

Silhouette Special Edition

Just Eight Months Old... #1362
The Woman for Dusty Conrad #1427
What a Woman Wants #1505
Where You Least Expect It #1600

Harlequin Blaze

You Sexy Thing! #15
A Stranger's Touch #37
Every Move You Make #56
Fire and Ice #65
Going Too Far #73
Night Fever #105
Flavor of the Month #109
Just Between Us... #113

Harlequin Temptation

Never Say Never Again #837
Private Investigations #876
Skin Deep #890
Red-Hot and Reckless #924

TORI CARRINGTON

is the pseudonym of award-winning husband-and-wife writing team Lori and Tony Karayianni. Twisting the old adage "life is stranger than fiction," they describe their lives as being "better than fiction." Since romance plays such a large role in their personal lives, it's only natural that romance fiction is what they would choose to write in their professional lives. Along with their four cats, they call Toledo, Ohio, home, but travel "home" to Greece as often as possible.

This prolific writing duo also writes for Harlequin Temptation and Harlequin Blaze under the Tori Carrington pseudonym. Lori and Tony love to hear from readers. Write to them at P.O. Box 12271, Toledo, OH 43612 for an autographed bookplate, or visit them on the Web at www.toricarrington.com, www.specialauthors.com or www.eHarlequin.com.

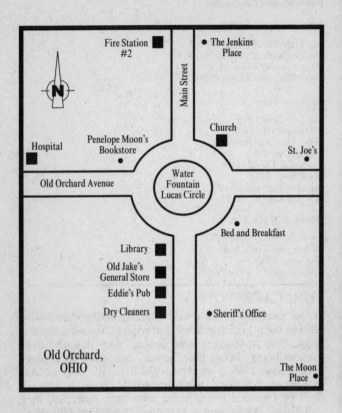

Fire Station #2

The Jenkins Place

Main Street

Church

Hospital

Penelope Moon's Bookstore

St. Joe's

Water Fountain Lucas Circle

Old Orchard Avenue

Bed and Breakfast

Library

Old Jake's General Store

Eddie's Pub

Dry Cleaners

Sheriff's Office

Old Orchard, OHIO

The Moon Place

Chapter One

Summer always had a way of making Penelope Moon itch. Maybe it was the heat. On this muggy, late-June morning, at just before eight, it was definitely hot. And it would only get hotter as the day went on.

She tugged on Maximus's leash while they walked down Main Street in downtown Old Orchard. The setter and Great Dane mix pulled back, nearly jerking her out of her practical sandals. She pulled tighter, smiling at Old Man Jake who was sweeping the sidewalk in front of his General Store. He gave her the same wary look he always gave her.

No, it wasn't the heat. Well, it was and it wasn't. Something else was to blame for the way she seemed to come alive in the summer, making her want to shuck her clothes and go skinny-dipping, an outrageous act that she would never give thought to at any other time of the year, in the Old Valley River near her grandmother's house. And that had nothing whatsoever to do with the weather in northwest Ohio.

Perhaps it was the extremeness of summer. The heat seemed to amplify every emotion, pump up the volume of sounds, make smells more intense, colors more vivid, overwhelming the senses.

Then again, maybe it was because she was a winter baby and the polar opposite, summer, mystified her.

"Max!" she whispered to the mammoth, untrained dog as he stopped in Lucas Circle in front of a half-barrel planted with red impatiens and started to lift his leg.

Penelope Moon was twenty-four, unmarried in a family with a history of unmarried women, and had taken over her grandmother's New Age bookstore five years ago. Back then, though, it hadn't been a bookstore but rather a general herb shop called Potions and Spells. To be fair, the herbs still sold better than the books, but somehow "Bookstore" in the name lent the shop a more suitable air and encouraged more foot traffic, no matter the customers' preferences.

Penelope still lived in the same house she'd grown up in, accepted that she would always be looked on as peculiar by the town, and appreciated every moment she stood above ground rather than lay buried in it. Heat and uneasiness aside, this morning pretty much resembled every other morning of her adult life. She got up just before dawn, made herself a cup of ginseng tea, watched the sunrise while sitting on the front porch of the old house she shared with her grandmother just outside of town. Then she put Maximus's leash on and walked the two miles to open the bookstore in downtown Old Orchard, where she would spend the next eight hours before heading back home to help her grandmother Mavis make dinner.

Penelope caught herself smoothing down the tiny hairs at the back of her neck, trying to calm her restlessness. A state that even the dog seemed to tune in to as he looked at her with his watery brown eyes and gave a small whine.

She resisted the urge to tell him to hush. The townspeople already thought her strange enough without witnessing her talking to her dog.

She took her keys out of the front pocket of her cotton dress and looked around the clump of businesses that sat, one against the other, down Main Street and Old Orchard Avenue. Eddie's Pub had already opened, but was likely serving coffee rather than beer this early. The library directly across from her was still closed. She could just make out some activity at the sheriff's office across Lucas Circle and down a ways.

The tiny brass bells in the shape of morning glories tinkled as she opened the glass door bearing her shop's name and hours in purple and white. The colors were mirrored inside with crisp, white wood bookcases lining the walls, and sprigs of lavender displayed everywhere.

Maximus gave a loud bark and pulled free of her grasp, galloping straight toward a waist-high display of aromatherapy lotions she had carefully stacked the day before.

"Max, no!" Penelope hurried after him, leaving the door unlocked behind her.

His leash was within reach, but it was too late. The four-foot pyramid of smooth, white plastic jars tumbled into a pile at her feet, one jar landing on her big toe.

"Ouch! Oh, Max."

She stood staring at the mess, then at the canine—who was looking pleased with himself as he sat next to the demolished mountain, his tongue lolling. She'd had the exasperating dog for two years and had yet to find a way to tame his roguish ways. A Scorpio. Definitely a Scorpio. Though she had no way of knowing for sure. She'd awakened in the middle of the night to find him howling on the front porch where someone had put him, little more than a pup. She'd taken the abandoned pooch under her wing before he could blink his mournful eyes. Penelope had never even tried to find out who had left him there. All that mattered was that he'd needed love and she'd had it to give to him.

If only she was any good at discipline, maybe her life with him wouldn't be so difficult. Even Mavis refused to keep him at the house while Penelope was at the shop.

"You," she said, rubbing his ear. "Out back."

"He ought to be put down, that dog."

Penelope turned from where she was gathering the jars in her arms to find town gossip Elva Mollenkopf in the door, wearing her normal drab clothes and familiar lemon-sucking expression.

I should have locked the door behind me, Penelope thought. She put the jars down on the checkout counter, pretending not to notice the way Elva tried to hide behind displays and the two purple poles flanking the entrance to conceal her presence in the shop from anyone passing outside.

"He's not that bad, really," Penelope said, giving the dog a beseeching look not to prove her wrong. "He's just a little clumsy is all."

"He's a menace."

Penelope raised a brow and forced a smile as she turned fully toward the other woman. Elva wasn't looking at her. Rather, she was trying to see whether she'd been spotted by anyone passing by.

"Drat that Lion's store. I don't know why they stopped carrying my face cream. It would be so much easier if I could still get it there."

Fewer covert maneuvers, Penelope agreed silently.

Of course, even Elva grudgingly admitted that the herbal cream she bought from Penelope's store was much more effective than the name-brand stuff she'd spent an arm and a leg on at the exclusive department store. In fact, during her last browsing expedition, Penelope was convinced she'd seen the face cream Elva claimed to have used right there on the cosmetics counter of the store in question. It was all she could do not to share the information with Elva. But no matter how much the woman bothered her, she needed the business.

Elva glanced over her shoulder from where she had a death grip on the foot-wide pole. "Did the cream come in?"

Penelope nodded. "Received a shipment from the guy in brown late yesterday."

"Thank God."

Elva released the pole and started toward the counter. "How much?"

Penelope named a price as she unlocked the register and put the prepared order on the glass countertop.

Elva's eyebrows rose to meet the poorly dyed black of her hair. "That much?"

"Same price every time you buy it, Mrs. Mollenkopf."

"I think you're wrong. Could you check, please?"

Penelope smiled at her. "Sure."

Out of the corner of her eye, she saw Maximus get to his feet, his tail wagging with mischievous intent as he rounded the counter. Elva gasped as he pressed his cold snout into her crotch. The calculated nature of his actions made Penelope catch her breath.

"Max!" Penelope grabbed hold of his leash and tried to pull him back, a completely inappropriate laugh erupting from her mouth. She quickly cleared her throat. "I'm sorry, Mrs. Mollenkopf. You know how dogs are."

"I loathe dogs and have never spent time around them, so no, Miss Moon, I would not know *how dogs are.*"

She should have caught a clue in the two years she'd been coming into the shop—but Penelope wasn't about to sass her.

"If you'd waited until I opened the store, Max would have been tied up out back." Terrorizing her business neighbors when they tried to throw something out in the Dumpster rather than burrowing his nose in other people's business.

Elva pulled the skirt of her dress out and stared at it in horror, as if she believed it permanently stained. "I'll have you know that I'm going to file a complaint with the sheriff's office."

So what else is new?

"Pardon me?"

Penelope blinked at the older woman as she finally managed to gain control of the dog and pull him back. She hadn't said the words, had she?

Maybe this morning was not like every other morning, after all.

"What if I give you a special ten-percent discount, Mrs. Mollenkopf?" she said. "You know, by way of apology for Max's behavior?"

"Fifteen."

"Done."

Max sat, and she ignored his expression—which seemed to say "sucker"—as she rounded the counter to complete the transaction.

"Strange, that man."

Penelope squinted at where Elva was staring through the front window at a figure walking down the street. The man's hands were in the pockets of his khaki pants; his crisp, white short-sleeved shirt emphasized his long, lean arms and the deep copper tone of his skin.

"I don't think Mr. Kendall's strange."

Elva glared at her. "Neither does the rest of the town. But I'm telling you, he's strange. Blows in here from out of nowhere a year ago, no family, no mention of a family, and becomes so much a part of the community, you can't tell him from the next guy."

"He's from Oregon. He doesn't have any family. And he's a middle-school teacher at St. Joe's. What more do you want to know?"

Elva looked at her a little too closely, then took

her change and counted it again. "I'd like to get a peek at what skeletons he's hiding in that closet of his over at Mrs. O'Malley's bed-and-breakfast." She lifted a finger after putting her money in a black-sequined change purse. "And that's another thing. Who lives in a bed-and-breakfast? A bed-and-breakfast is where one spends a weekend, not a year."

Penelope said, "I'm sure there are no skeletons in Mr. Kendall's closet, Mrs. Mollenkopf."

"Shows how much you know."

Penelope handed the woman the bag of cream just as the door bells rang, heralding another customer. She hadn't even opened for business. She wondered why it couldn't be this busy during the regular workday.

"Good morning, Miss Moon." Aidan Kendall, the topic of their conversation, came inside, seeming to bring the sun with him. "Mrs. Mollenkopf."

"Harrumph," Elva said, sticking her nose in the air and stalking toward the door.

Aidan opened it for her, and she sailed through without so much as a "thank you" or an "excuse me."

"Careful, Mrs. Mollenkopf, or I might get the impression that you don't like me very much," Aidan said in good humor.

She made another sound of disapproval, looked both ways down the street, then hurried away, probably praying she hadn't been seen coming out of the shop. At least until the town cat, Spot, crossed her path, nearly tripping her. The fearless female feline ducked into the shop before the door could close. Max tilted his head to the side and made an inquisitive noise as if unable to believe a cat had just offered itself up for a morning snack. He leaned forward from where he sat in the storage room. Penelope easily closed the door, shutting him in, then moved to continue picking up the jars of fallen cream.

"Was it something I said?" Aidan asked, aiming a thumb at Elva's quickly retreating back.

Penelope wondered why her skin suddenly seemed to burn all the hotter. "I wouldn't take her behavior, um, personally. She doesn't appear to like anybody much."

Aidan bent to pat Spot as she made a perfect figure eight around his ankles, even as he gazed at Penelope. "Yeah."

Her skin grew hotter still. Much hotter than she was comfortable with.

Darn summer and its heat.

She put the next load of jars down on the counter, then moved to the thermostat to switch on the air-conditioning. "Looks like it's going to be another scorcher."

"I like it hot."

Penelope suddenly had a hard time swallowing.

Aidan Kendall liked hot weather.

She slowly turned to find him picking up the jars.

"No!" she fairly shouted.

His puzzled expression made her wince.

"I mean, you don't have to do that. Really, you don't." She hurried over to take the jars out of his hands. "I have plenty of time to take care of it before I open up."

Aidan stood still, allowing her to take the jars from him. Only, his arms could hold much more than hers. She juggled hers as he held up the last one, his grin making her toes curl inside her sandals.

"Just trying to help," he said.

She looked at him and found herself leisurely staring into his deep brown eyes, noticing the slight crinkles at the corners, taking in the broad, manly curve of his jaw, the sensual definition of his lips. She wasn't sure what it was, but she felt restless when he was around. All it took was one glance from him. He threw off an energy that messed with her own calm, making her not only want to peel off her clothes, but climb out of her own skin.

Which would be all right, if only she didn't itch to try on his skin instead.

Penelope unloaded the jars. "Is there, um, something you wanted, Aidan?"

He shrugged and slipped his hands back into his pockets. "Isn't it enough to want to stop and say hello to a friend?"

A friend.

Penelope fingered the smooth lid of a jar she held and considered the word. Such a simple word, really. But not one she had come across often in her lifetime in Old Orchard.

She'd never really had any friends. Her peers and the rest of the townsfolk had always seemed more like wary strangers.

Except for Aidan.

Every now and again he would pop up into her shop, giving her those curious toe-curling looks and trying to strike up conversation.

She smiled at him. "It's more than enough."

"Good, because it's not the reason why I stopped by."

She gave a tiny giggle.

A giggle? She didn't giggle. The sound was so unfamiliar to her that she caught herself looking around to make sure someone else hadn't entered the shop.

She cleared her throat, thinking that she really needed to get a grip.

Aidan felt all the tension seep from his muscles. He enjoyed Penelope Moon's laugh. There was something genuine about the musical sound. Something that reached out and grabbed him unaware, reminding him of what was light and happy rather than dark and sad.

There was also an innocence about her that

made him feel good. When he was around her, he forgot the reason he'd first come to this small town in the middle of nowhere and allowed himself to be, well, basically himself. She didn't ask questions of him. Didn't pressure him for details he was loath to give. She merely accepted him for the man that stood in front of her.

She was also a sight for jaded eyes.

Oh, he knew what the rest of the townspeople said about her. The nicest thing they said was that she was a bit odd. The worst, that she was a practicing witch—one you didn't want to cross lest she cast a spell on you. The latter had come from Mrs. Mollenkopf herself the other day. He'd overheard her in the post office when he'd gone to buy a book of stamps.

He supposed Penelope Moon did look the part, what with her long, silky black hair and big black eyes and pale skin. But rather than see her as odd, he preferred to think of her as real. As real as anyone he'd met since his late wife.

"Leo."

Aidan blinked, realizing Penelope had said something. "Pardon me?"

"Your sun sign. You're a Leo, right?"

He cracked a grin. He should have known what she'd meant straight off. She'd been asking him to give her his birth date since the first day they met. When he'd refused, she'd taken to trying to guess his sign.

Just as he always did, he shook his head. "Not a Leo."

Her soft mouth turned down into a frown that merely enhanced her natural beauty. She didn't have on even a touch of lipstick, but her lips were still the deep, ripe color of strawberries in season. He'd bet she didn't wear mascara, either, even though her lashes were thick and sweeping, and vividly outlined her dark, dark eyes.

She cocked her head as she looked at him looking at her. "If I got your sun sign right, would you admit it?"

He slowly shook his head. "No."

"Taurus."

He chuckled. "No."

He didn't want to think about the truth behind his hesitancy. The fact was, he couldn't give her his real birth date for fear of what might happen in the future. And he didn't want to lie to her either.

Better to keep things light between them.

He watched her touch a leather band holding a charm—one he couldn't make out—around her slim wrist.

"So, you said there was a reason you came in here?" she said quietly. Too quietly.

Aidan blinked and looked up into her fathomless eyes. "Um, yes. I wondered why I didn't see you at the Fourth of July planning committee meeting last night."

She broke the connection of their gazes as she looked down. "Hmm...I don't know. Maybe because I'm not a member of the planning committee?"

She moved toward the mess of jars all over the floor and bent to continue picking them up.

She was slender. Almost too slender. Easily as tall as he was at five foot eleven, her limbs were long and willowy, almost model-like. Or they would be if she wore more flattering clothes. Instead she leaned toward muted earth-tone dresses that he guessed to be a size or two too big. It was at moments like these, however, when she was bent, forcing the fabric to mold to her body, that he noticed how very curvy she was.

And was reminded of how long it had been since he was with a woman.

"I see," he said, crouching to help her. "So the meeting conflicted with another committee meeting, maybe?"

She looked at him shyly. "No."

"Ah. So the reason has to be a man, then."

Her flush was so complete, so unexpected, that his stomach knotted.

"Um, the answer to that would have to be no, as well."

Aidan's chest tightened. Over the past twelve months he'd come to see that this woman had so very much to give...if only she could be encouraged to do so. Her opinions were fresh and unbiased. Her appearance uplifting. Her very presence like a spring breeze.

He hated to watch her go back and forth from her grandmother's house to her shop, never stopping to talk to anyone, never veering from the well-tread course, never batting an eye when on occasion the town kids would call her the witch that so many of them believed her to be.

He'd thought if he could get her to come out of her shop, upset her normal pattern, force the town to see her for who she really was, he would be doing her—and them—a favor.

And if a small fringe benefit was that he would have an excuse to spend more time around her, he wasn't going to acknowledge it. Of course, he couldn't allow himself to get involved with her. Or anyone else for that matter. Not until he could take care of some very important issues on his personal agenda.

She whispered something.

"Pardon me?" he asked.

She blinked at him, seeming horrified. "I didn't say anything."

"I could have sworn…" She looked utterly aghast, and he realized that whatever she'd said hadn't been meant to be heard. He smiled. "Never mind." He leaned back on his heels and handed her the jars one by one, while she reached up to place them on the counter. "Anyway, the holiday is only a week away and the committee is no closer to agreeing on a theme than they were three months ago. I could really use an ally.'' He offered up a grin. ''Someone whose vote I could count on. Besides, acting like a member of the community might be a good idea.''

Her eyes narrowed a bit as she continued taking the jars from him. ''I've been a member of this community my entire life.''

''That's not what I meant.''

He refused to release his grip on the last jar. She held on to it even as he did. He swore he felt a strange warmth climb up his arm and down into his stomach.

''I know,'' she said finally.

Aidan moved his fingers until they were covering hers. Her skin was so soft, so warm and inviting under his. He'd forgotten what it was like to touch a woman in that simple yet intimate way. Forgotten how alive it made him feel.

The bells above the door jingled, shattering the moment. He released the jar. Penelope's flush deepened as she put it on the counter, then she rose.

''Good morning, Sheriff Parker.''

A jolt of fear shot through Aidan as he got to his feet.

He reminded himself that he had nothing to fear from Sheriff Cole Parker.

At least, not yet…

Chapter Two

If Penelope had felt restless before, Aidan's brief touch upgraded the emotion to chaos. A heart-stopping awareness that toyed with her body temperature and cut the bottom out of her stomach, made her feel like a stranger to herself.

Oh, she'd always thought Aidan attractive. Very attractive. But she had never before linked herself to him in the same sentence, as in "Aidan and I." She hadn't dared.

Now her mind was going a million miles a minute doing just that.

He smiled at her as if he knew what she was thinking, and her pulse leaped.

"I just came by for some more of that tea you made for me the other day, Penelope," Sheriff Parker was saying as he took off his hat. "I usually don't go in for that kind of stuff, but, well, I liked it."

It seemed to take a great deal of effort to tug her gaze away from Aidan's face. "Sure. I'll just put some water on to boil."

"Sheriff." She heard Aidan greet the other man as she plugged in her electric teapot, then eyed the tins of herbal teas on the shelf behind her. For the life of her, she couldn't remember what tea she had fixed for Cole.

"Aidan," Cole said back.

"How's everything across the Circle this morning? Any new crimes to report?"

A simple question. But when an answer wasn't immediately forthcoming, Penelope looked over her shoulder to find Cole running his fingers through his hair, obviously troubled.

"Funny you should ask that. Something strange did happen last night."

Penelope settled on green tea with a hint of ginseng and measured a few spoonfuls into a small teapot. She turned to put some prepackaged raspberry biscuits onto a plate, tuning in to an odd kind of tension emanating from Cole. He seemed to be eyeing Aidan in a curious way.

Cole finally sighed. "Old Man Smythe's filling

station was hit last night. He was robbed at gun-point.''

Aidan was in the act of accepting a biscuit when—Penelope could have sworn—his hand hesitated. ''Nobody was hurt, I hope?''

''No, no one was hurt. But Smythe did give an interesting description of the assailant. He said he looked exactly like you—'' The sheriff rubbed the back of his neck, then lapsed into silence as the kettle began to whistle.

Penelope turned to pour hot water into the pot. ''Actually, his exact words were 'that school-teacher Kendall robbed me.'''

Penelope nearly knocked over the teapot. She turned to watch the two men stare at each other.

Then, finally, Cole chuckled.

''Yeah, I figured the old man was overdue for a visit with the optometrist.''

She handed Cole his tea and offered a cup to Aidan, as well.

''Thanks, Penelope.'' Cole blew on the liquid, then took a sip. ''Ah, heaven.'' He smiled at her. ''You wouldn't happen to have a package of this stuff I could buy, would you?''

''No, that's my own personal stash,'' she said, then laughed. ''Of course I do. How much would you like?''

The next ten minutes or so were filled with light talk of what else was going on in town and wrapping up Cole's purchases. Finally, Cole put his hat back on, accepted another cup of tea in a disposable cup and bid them a good day.

The tinkling of the bells seemed to echo through the shop for a long time after he left.

"Imagine, Mr. Smythe thinking you were the one who robbed him," she said, wiping the counter.

Aidan didn't appear to hear her. His expression was somber and thoughtful as his gaze fixed on the sheriff's office across Lucas Circle.

"How much do I owe you for the tea?" he asked absently.

Penelope blinked. "It's on the house, Aidan."

He peeled off a couple of dollars and put them on the counter. "I'll see you later."

Penelope watched him leave, noticing that Spot followed him out with a brief glance in her direction. She felt more than a little disappointed. Had she imagined what had passed between them before Cole had come in? Dreamed that his fingers had lain on top of hers for a brief moment, making time stop?

She swallowed. Silly, really. Thinking a man like Aidan Kendall could be interested in her.

She opened the storage room door, then took Max's leash in hand and set about her normal everyday chores, telling herself she would do well to remember the town was divided into two very distinct camps: her…and everyone else.

And it seemed "everyone else" included Aidan Kendall.

* * *

He'd stayed in town too long.

Later that day, after seeing the summer school students off with just enough homework to make them groan, Aidan headed back to his room at Mrs. O'Malley's.

What a difference one sentence could make in a man's life. A few simple words said by someone with the power to make them damning.

He should never have come to Old Orchard at all. And he definitely should have left six months ago when the teacher he had temporarily replaced returned from maternity leave.

Aidan let himself into Mrs. O'Malley's bed-and-breakfast, grateful she was in the kitchen preparing dinner and didn't notice him come in. She usually wanted to know about his day, and he usually enjoyed watching her face light up as he shared student anecdotes, and reports on how they were all doing.

He hated to imagine what expression she would wear when she found out who he really was.

He climbed the stairs and unlocked the door to his room at the far end of the hall, then closed it behind him. Since he was a semipermanent boarder, he'd offered to look after his own things. At least, that had been his excuse. In reality, he didn't think it was a good idea for Mrs. O'Malley to know what all was going on in here. He stood in the middle of the large room. To his left two computers were set up on the old antique desk, one running on a separate cable line and doing a continual search on news articles across the country. The other, an older system he used to compile the data he received. Next to the desk were stacks upon stacks of newspapers he subscribed to and picked up from a post office box he rented in a neighboring county.

In one year he'd come up with nothing.

In one day he'd come up with everything.

Davin had finally caught up with him...

Aidan sat down on the bed and dropped his head into his hands as if trying to hold everything in. An image of Penelope Moon's pretty face flashed across his mind.

Penelope.

He'd been selfish. Selfish to think he'd be safe here. Selfish to make himself a part of a community that could be hurt merely by being associated with him. Selfish to want a woman who deserved so much better than what he had to offer her.

He slid open the drawer in the bedside table and took out a five-by-seven frame. The glass was dusty. He wiped it off and stared down into the faces of his wife and his three-year-old son. Two people lost to him forever. Two people who had also deserved better than him, because he'd been unable to protect them.

He slid the backing from the frame and took out

the photo behind the one of his wife and son. It was a studio portrait taken some twenty-two years ago, when he was eight. A picture taken of him and his identical twin brother, Davin. A picture taken before his mother had suffered a beating that had nearly killed her and his father was sentenced to two years in prison for felonious assault. A picture taken before both his parents died in a house fire when he and Davin were fourteen.

Before everything in their lives that had already been bad had gotten even worse.

There was a brief knock at the door. "Aidan?"

He slid the photographs into place, then put the frame back and closed the drawer. Within moments, he stood looking at Mrs. O'Malley from the open doorway.

She smiled at him. "I thought I heard footsteps on the stairs. Why didn't you come into the kitchen to say hello?"

In the corner the computer made a small *beep* indicating the search had found something. They both looked at it.

"Always working," Mrs. O'Malley said.

At one time Edith O'Malley herself had been a ninth grade English teacher. She'd retired ten years ago following the death of her husband, then transformed their family home into a bed-and-breakfast long after her five children had left Old Orchard for busier concrete pastures. Once Mrs. O'Malley had learned that Aidan was certified as a schoolteacher, she had secured the job for him at St. Joseph's with nary a background check. Mrs. O'Malley trusted him completely, based on instinct, as she didn't understand computers and never invaded his privacy.

Mrs. O'Malley's smile slowly faded as she looked into his face now.

"Is everything all right, Aidan? You don't look well."

He cleared his throat. "Actually, I am feeling a bit tired, Mrs. O'Malley. Sorry I didn't say hello, but I had my hands full of class materials and wanted to bring them up here first."

The smile made a return. "You'll come down for dinner, though, won't you? Tonight's meat loaf night."

He foraged around for a smile to offer in return. "I wouldn't dream of missing meat loaf night."

"Good," she said, nodding, leaning on her cane to turn around in the hall. A cane she used only now and again when, as she said, her new hip went to war with her old one. "I'll see you in twenty minutes, then."

"Twenty minutes."

He watched her carefully navigate the steps, thinking that if he knew what was good for them all, he would be long gone in ten.

Penelope closed the wood gate, its white paint worn off by time and weather, and released Maximus's lead. Of course, the moment he was free, he plopped down at her feet, his tongue forever lolling as he gazed up at her.

She patted his head. "A Gemini. Definitely a Gemini."

She heard pounding coming from inside the one-story house with the wide, slanting front porch and headed for the steps. She and her grandmother Mavis Moon had lived there alone since Penelope's mother died when she was five. And seeing as neither one of them had much skill when it came to repairs, the house and surrounding yard needed a lot of them.

"Gram? I'm home," she called out as the old screen door squeaked, then slapped shut behind her.

She heard mumbling coming from the dining room, then, "Of course you're home. Where else would you be at this time of day? It's five-thirty and you're home. Shocker."

Penelope put her bag of leftover raspberry biscuits in the kitchen and headed for the doorway to the dining room, puzzled by Mavis's comments. "Did you say something?"

Her grandmother waved her away with the hammer she held. Slender, she looked almost too weak to wield such a heavy object. Especially given the flowing purple tunic that billowed around her petite frame like a circus tent.

Penelope slowly entered the room, her gaze riveted to the pictures of her mother Mavis had framed and positioned willy-nilly.

"What do you think?" Mavis asked, seeming to challenge her with her dark eyes.

"Um, it's nice," Penelope said though she was overwhelmed with images of her mother staring back at her from dozens of angles.

She stepped forward to straighten a crooked frame.

"Don't touch that," her grandmother said, seeming to threaten injury with the hammer if Penelope moved another inch. "Everything is exactly where I want it."

"Okay," Penelope said carefully. "I'll, um, just go in and start dinner."

Had the whole world gone nuts while she wasn't looking? First Aidan had come into her shop looking at her like she was a desirable woman. Then Sheriff Parker had said Mr. Smythe had identified Aidan as the man who had robbed him. Then she'd returned home to find her normally tranquil grandmother pounding the heck out of the dining room wall, instead of relaxing in a yoga stance.

She looked around on the sparkling clean countertops of the kitchen, inside the empty oven, then in the refrigerator. Aside from a half-empty pitcher of lemonade, there wasn't a crumb to be found.

Where was the ground turkey she had taken out of the freezer and put in the refrigerator to defrost this morning? The fresh salad fixings? Even her homemade yogurt was missing.

"I got rid of it all," Mavis said, dropping the hammer onto the counter with a loud *thud*. "All of it. It was messing with my biorhythms."

"What did you do with it?" Penelope asked.

"Threw it away, of course. All of it."

Penelope caught herself absently rubbing her stomach where it growled. Biscuits aside, she hadn't had a thing to eat all day and her body was letting her know about it.

Out of the corner of her eye she watched her grandmother approach the counter where she'd put the biscuits.

"Don't you dare!" she said, taking the bag from the older woman. She rolled the top of the bag back up, put it on the table closer to her and propped her hand on her hip. "Did you stop taking your medication again?"

Her grandmother waved a bony hand. "Medication, shmedication. I threw it all out with the rest of it."

Dread drifted through Penelope as she headed to check the rest of the house. As an afterthought, she returned to the table and snatched up the bag of biscuits, her dinner if she didn't go out and pick anything else up.

Ten minutes later she'd verified her suspicions: Mavis had thrown away everything in the medicine cabinets, including her doctor-prescribed medications and toothpaste, as well as all the cleaners and detergents under the sink and in the broom closet.

Penelope stood dumbfounded, unable to make heads or tails out of the situation.

Well, at least she'd left the garden out back alone. The crooked rows of young vegetable plants were coming along nicely. In fact, it appeared Mavis had even weeded and watered them.

She made her way back into the dining room, where her grandmother was starting on the second wall.

"Have you eaten anything at all today?" she asked.

Mavis waved her hand. "Who needs food?"

"Last I checked? I don't know. Maybe you?"

"I don't want anything."

"Then, maybe I should call the hospital and ask them to hold a room for you, because that's where you'll be heading if you don't eat something." She glanced toward the living room. "Unless, of course, you've thrown the telephone out too?"

Mavis stared at her.

Penelope swallowed hard. "No, I'm not talking about the psychiatric ward."

"I didn't say you were."

"You didn't have to."

Mavis climbed down off the stepladder and turned toward her. "Don't you ever get sick of it all, Popi?"

It had been a long time since her grandmother

had called her the pet name. Her doing so now opened up a soft spot inside Penelope. When she was young, she'd thought it meant something pope-like. Important. She'd found out later that it was merely a Greek shortening of her name.

"I mean, the sameness of everything? We get up at the same time every morning—"

"So, sleep in."

"We eat dinner at the same time every night—"

"So, we'll eat later."

"We talk to the same people, do the same things—"

"So, we'll go out and meet new people, do different things."

Mavis looked a breath away from hitting her with the hammer again. "Can't I even have a nervous breakdown without you being so damn calm about everything?"

Penelope smiled. "No."

Her grandmother hit the wall with the hammer and Penelope jumped.

Mavis examined her handiwork. "I like it."

Penelope rolled her eyes, wondering how much work she would have to do when her grandmother's mood ended this time.

This wasn't the first time Mavis Moon had done something *extreme*, even by Penelope's own generous definition of the word. About once a year Penelope would come home to find her grandmother acting strangely. The last time Mavis had planted a crop of marijuana in with the corn out back, determined to do for terminally ill patients what the health care system wouldn't.

It was all Penelope could do to stop her from being charged. She had, however, been arrested.

She let out a long breath. "I'm going to the store. Do you want anything?"

"A man."

Penelope stared at her grandmother's back.

"I can feel you looking at me, girl. Stop it right now."

"Where would you have me look?"

"Oh, I don't know. Maybe at yourself in the mirror." She gave the wall another smack, creating another ugly dent. She gestured with the hammer. "You and me…we're not getting any younger, you know. This morning I swore I could hear time passing."

"It was probably your pacemaker."

Mavis glared at her.

"Do you want anything from the market?"

"I told you what I want."

"And short of dragging Old Man Jake home with me, it's not going to happen."

A thoughtful expression came over her grandmother's face. Penelope turned on her heel, collected Max's leash and went out the front door.

She only hoped that there would be a house to return to.

Chapter Three

What could have been minutes or hours later, Penelope stood on the old wooden bridge about a half-mile away, down the road that spanned the Old Valley River. She stared at the water rushing by below and pondered why every now and again life didn't make any sense at all. Even Max seemed to contemplate the question, lying on the old planks under their feet that shuddered whenever a car drove over. Which, thankfully, wasn't often.

Penelope had studied the stars last night, trying to map out the future, catch a clue on where things might be heading. The same way she did every other night when there was no significant cloud cover. Only nothing had prepared her for today. She'd seen no hint of Mavis' latest mood. No sign that she would look into Aidan's eyes that morning and feel a tingling awareness that she hadn't been able to shake ever since. No trace that she would be standing at the bridge now, staring down at the river wondering if things would have been different if her mother hadn't committed suicide by jumping off the other side of this same bridge and landing on the outcropping of rocks there.

The early evening sunlight hit her full on the back and seemed to outline her reflection in the water. She couldn't make out her own features. The blurry image resembled what little she could remember about her mother's features beyond those she saw in the countless photos Mavis had of her.

After Heather Moon died, no more photographs were brought into the house. Penelope couldn't even remember seeing the old camera her mother had once owned. Maybe Mavis had buried it with her.

She recalled the way Mavis had mapped out the old photographs on the wall like some sort of puzzle missing half its pieces, or like a map leading to nowhere. She shivered.

"Cold?"

She looked up, startled to find she was no longer alone.

Aidan stood on the bridge next to her. He had

probably been there for a while, given his relaxed stance next to her. He too was staring into the water.

"No, I, um…"

Her voice drifted off as she realized the question was probably rhetorical. She smiled. "I think you're about the last person I expected to see way out here."

Aidan shrugged, his forearms leaning against the broad wood railing, his strong, masculine hands clasped tightly together. She couldn't be sure, but given the grooves on either side of his mouth, he had been thinking heavy thoughts too.

She squinted at him, remembering the first time she saw him ten months or so ago. He'd been walking down the street outside her shop, much as he did every morning. But back then he had looked more anxious somehow. Terribly alone. And his brown eyes had held a sadness that seemed to reach out and clutch her heart.

She remembered it so clearly because she was seeing the same expression now.

"I went out for a walk after dinner and lost track of time," he said by way of explanation.

Look at me, Penelope silently found herself saying.

"Did you say something?"

He finally looked at her, and the full impact of the soulless shadow in his eyes nearly took her breath away.

Max barked, startling them both, then laid his head back down on top of his paws.

"No," Penelope said quietly. "I didn't say anything."

Although, it was the second time that day that he had appeared to hear her thoughts.

The first time she had silently willed him to kiss her.

She felt her face go hot, then she turned back toward the water and tucked her hair behind her ear. "You know, my mother used to say that there are only a few people in the world who are capable of hearing another's thoughts." Actually, her mother had told her that there would be one other person capable of hearing her thoughts, and that one person would be the one she was meant to spend her life with. But she wasn't going to say that to Aidan for fear that he would think her strange. Most of the townspeople already thought that. She couldn't bear it if he believed the same.

"My... There was another woman who told me that once." Aidan said it so quietly that the light breeze that had kicked up nearly stole the words before they reached her ears.

Penelope shivered again, but this time it had nothing to do with a chill, but rather a burst of heat.

She pushed from the railing and looked down at her watch. It was already after seven. "I didn't realize it was getting so late."

"Do you have a date?"

Penelope laughed, then stopped when she realized he was serious. "No. I don't have a date. I, um, was just heading to the market to pick up a few things." *And a man for my grandmother,* she reminded herself.

Maximus lumbered to his feet, nudging his cold, slimy nose into her hand. She absently patted him, then picked up his leash.

"I'll walk back with you," Aidan said.

"Okay."

They'd gone a ways, Max keeping pace between them, when suddenly the tree-lined route curved into a two-lane street and the trees morphed into buildings.

Aidan looked at Penelope walking leisurely beside him. It had been a long time since he'd been with someone who didn't demand that every second be filled with conversation.

But Penelope...

"What?"

He blinked, realizing she'd grown aware of his attention and was even now playing with her leather bracelet in that way she did when she was nervous.

He shook his head and smiled. "Nothing. I was just thinking that I never did get a straight answer to the question I asked this morning at the shop."

She seemed to think back to that morning, when

they'd shared that heated moment of awareness. But the image of the sheriff eyeing him suspiciously wiped it out of Aidan's mind.

"What question?"

"Hmm? Oh. Well, since I could really use some help with putting together the Fourth of July town celebration, would you consider coming to the next meeting? It's tomorrow night."

Her gaze flitted away and she fell silent.

"At the rate things are going, we'll end up with something that could have been cut and pasted from the 1950s. I could really use someone to back me up, help me urge everyone into the new millennium."

She still didn't say anything.

"Is everything okay?" He leaned forward to capture her gaze.

She smiled, but there was no happiness there. "Sure. Why wouldn't it be?"

"It's just that you got awfully quiet there for a moment."

"I was just thinking…"

What? What had she been thinking?

Aidan refused to speak the question aloud, but he found he was curious about Penelope in a way he hadn't been curious about a woman in a long time. While capable of walking in companionable silence with her for long stretches, he was filled with a desire to reach out and touch her, to urge out whatever it was she was holding in her mind...in her heart.

They'd come to a slow halt, a block short of the General Store. Max sat down, panting while Penelope turned to Aidan. To thank him for his company? More than likely. But she hesitated when she looked into his face.

What was there? he wondered. What did she see?

He found himself reaching out to cup her chin. Just a gentle play of his fingertips up along the delicate line of her jaw. So soft. She blinked those big dark eyes, appearing startled yet curious as her tongue darted out and moistened her lips.

Lips that Aidan wanted more than anything to kiss.

And in the next instant, he was doing just that.

First there was the welcoming shock of skin against skin, his lips pressing against hers, tenderly, tentatively.

He'd closed his eyes, but he opened them now to see that she watched him through a fringe of black lashes. He read fear, surprise and a wistful yearning that shot straight through him. His throat tightened to the point of pain, and a craving for this woman, so urgent, so overwhelming swept over him, paralyzing him with its unexpected power.

"Mmm," she whispered. "That was nice."

Aidan had experienced his share of kisses, and

what they had just shared was definitely not simply "nice." It was honest. It was sweet. And it was hot.

He stepped back away from her even as a voice deep inside him protested the move.

What was he doing?

He'd promised long ago that he would not involve anyone else in his problems. Would not subject them to what he had lived with for so long that it seemed as natural as the shadow that followed him. Especially since everything finally seemed to be coming to a head.

Yet a few minutes with Penelope found him shoving all that aside, left him seeking a bit of something outside himself. Something that called out to him from her.

He remembered her on the bridge when he'd first walked across to stand next to her. Her expression had spoken of a woman with secrets that seemed to run as deep as his. And he found himself feeling connected to her in a way he hadn't felt connected to anyone in a long time.

Only, Penelope's secrets didn't have the power to hurt others.

She laughed nervously. "I'd...better get going before the store closes."

Aidan blinked at her, wondering how long they'd been standing there looking at each other. What others thought didn't concern him. But what Penelope thought did matter. Maybe a little too much.

He offered a smile. "You still didn't answer my question."

She wrapped the end of Max's lead around her hand. "What question?"

"Whether you'll help me out with the Fourth of July celebration."

She fell silent again, but it wasn't a companionable silence this time, but rather a tense one. He silently berated himself for making her uncomfortable. Of pressing her to do something she so obviously didn't want to do. Especially since he didn't know if he would be here in town much longer.

"I can't," she said simply.

Aidan slid his hands into his pants pockets, reluctantly accepting her answer.

"I'd better go," she said.

Aidan found himself reaching out to lightly grasp her wrist. She looked back at him, curious, questioning.

"I'm…" he began.

The only sounds were of traffic farther up the street and of Max panting patiently at Penelope's side.

"I'm not who you think I am, Penelope," he found himself admitting.

She smiled as she reached out to hold his hand. "Right now, I'm not sure I know who anyone is, Aidan."

Chapter Four

Penelope lay awake late into the night, stretched across the twin bed that used to belong to her mother, thinking about Aidan and his words. And, even more acutely, her own words.

What had made her say what she said? That she wasn't sure she knew who anyone was anymore?

She caught her fingertips lingering against her lips and yanked her hand back to her side, then turned over, trying to ignore the incessant hammering coming from the next room. She'd returned from the General Store with the makings of spinach pasta, but Grammy hadn't touched a bit of it, too consumed with her house renovations. Penelope sighed.

Life in Old Orchard had always been trying for her. Still, there wasn't anything she could do to change it, so why bother trying? From what she understood, her mother had fought the same losing battle...until giving up the fight in a very real way.

Suddenly she realized that she could hear crickets instead of a hammer pounding away. She propped herself up onto her elbows, bunching the simple white nightgown she wore around her waist. What was Grammy doing now?

Footsteps in the hall, then the sound of her grandmother's bedroom door being slammed. Penelope collapsed onto the pillows, glad the old woman had finally called it a night. Maybe, just maybe, she'd be able to get some sleep tonight.

She rolled over to her other side and stared through the open window. The white sheers shifted in the light breeze, creating a ghostly atmosphere.

A drop of sweat trickled beneath the white cotton of her nightgown. The click of her swallowing sounded strangely amplified in the suddenly quiet room. She couldn't really say if she'd ever actually heard herself swallow before. Or had ever been so acutely aware of herself on every level. From the agitated state of her own emotions, to the trembling of her lips even now when Aidan had kissed her hours ago.

She then rolled over onto her back, wondering

if Aidan was having trouble sleeping across town at the bed-and-breakfast. Was he thinking about her the same way she was thinking about him? She honestly couldn't say. She'd never experienced what she was feeling now. It seemed like a heated awareness swam through her veins along with her blood, making her dizzy and giddy and remarkably...

She fought to put the feeling into words.

Afraid.

She held her breath for a moment, recognizing the emotion for what it was. She was afraid that she had imagined the desire that had passed between her and Aidan. Scared that the feelings growing within her weren't something she could ignore or explain away. Terrified that she was finally getting a taste of what it felt like to be in love.

Not that she thought she was in love with Aidan. She wasn't. Not yet, anyway.

She wondered what he could possibly want from her. He was a respected schoolteacher at the most respected school in Old Orchard. And she was the dark girl who lived on the outskirts of town and ran that odd shop across Lucas Square from the sheriff's office. Always was, always would be.

To date Aidan...

The sheets rustled as she turned over yet again. Wasn't she putting the cart a bit before the horse? Aidan hadn't even asked her out. But if he had...

If he had, she would have turned him down. Simply because he had everything to lose by being seen with her. And she...well, didn't dating someone open up the possibility of marriage somewhere down the road? While not every couple that dated ended up at the altar, certainly they didn't go into any dating situation knowing they never *intended* to stand at an altar.

And she'd always known she wasn't destined for the traditional institution of marriage. Had even begun to guess that she'd inherited a degenerate gene or two from the women before her. All she knew about her own father was that he'd been a traveling salesman and that he didn't even know she existed. And since her mother hadn't put his name on her birth certificate, she couldn't look for him. Her mother hadn't known her father either. She'd once joked that they could be a long lost branch from an Amazonian tribe. Grammy had not been amused and had said that the reason there were no men around was that they didn't *need* any men.

Lucky for all of them, then, that all the children born were female.

Her eyes widened. They had all been female, hadn't they? There wasn't a male out there somewhere rejected because of his gender, was there?

She frowned at the stupid idea, a thought she wouldn't even have considered just yesterday. But in twenty-four short hours it seemed the entire world had gone insane.

Okay, maybe not the entire world. But surely the Moon family had lost a marble or two or three.

Then there was Aidan and his reason for kissing her... She rolled over yet again. She needed to stop thinking about Aidan and get some sleep. She had a feeling she would need it....

Across town, Aidan was doing the exact same thing Penelope was, although minus one ornery grandmother to make his task more difficult.

The only light in the room came from the glowing computer screen that continued its programmed search for articles matching his search parameters. The windows of his room faced the backyard of the bed-and-breakfast, so no artificial light filtered through the light sheers. And given the moonless state of the sky, neither did any natural light.

A quiet *beep*. Aidan turned his head where it rested on his folded hands and stared at the computer screen.

He tossed off the top sheet and padded across the bare wood floor to have a look. A newspaper from a neighboring county had uploaded its latest stories, and one of them was on the robbery at Smythe's gas station. He clicked the mouse and read through it, but found no more information than Cole had offered.

He stretched to his full height and ran his hand through his tousled hair, unable to shake the uneasiness creeping through him like a shadowy mist.

Were his suspicions that Davin had found him true? Or was he allowing his imagination to run away with him? But he was a man who never gave much credence to coincidences. Even if Old Man Smythe needed to have his glasses prescription upgraded, one didn't lightly make the kind of accusation that he had.

He crossed back to the bed and sat down on it, the old springs giving a soft *squeak*. Of course, his uneasiness couldn't be blamed solely on his suspicions. No, if he were to be completely honest with himself, Penelope Moon had a great deal to do with his current restless state.

He closed his eyes and groaned, remembering their kiss earlier. She'd tasted so sweet. Her lips had been so soft. Her body as she briefly swayed against him, so inviting.

He still wasn't altogether sure why he'd kissed her. He'd merely had an urge to press his mouth against hers. Partly because she'd looked like she'd wanted it so much. Mostly because he had wanted it so much.

He reached to switch on the lamp, his hand nearly knocking something over. He quickly caught the object, then switched on the light. A glass of milk and a small plate of freshly baked double-chocolate oatmeal cookies sat next to his alarm clock. He smiled faintly. Mrs. O'Malley must have sneaked in to leave the snack when he was in the shower. He'd been so distracted he hadn't even noticed until now.

Penelope. Mrs. O'Malley. Everyone he'd met since coming to Old Orchard. He could only imagine their disappointment when they discovered his true identity.

Perhaps it would be best if they never found out....

He glanced around the room that had become home to him in the past year. It had always been homey, but that was more Mrs. O'Malley's doing than his. Gold-framed oil paintings hung on the walls, the sheer curtains were handmade. The white throw rug with tiny pink and purple flowers complimented the quilt across the foot of the hulking oak bed. The only objects that were his were the computers, the newspapers in a pile next to the rolltop desk, and the dress shirt he'd draped over the back of the chair. Everything else was tucked into the walk-in closet.

It made him sad to know that within five minutes he would be set to leave—which didn't make much sense since he'd planned it that way.

He got up and stepped to the closet, careful not to make much noise as he hoisted the empty leather suitcase from the top shelf, then placed it across the bed. In went his suits, his clothes and a few other personal items. He left out only those things he would need in the morning.

Ten minutes later he sat on the bed looking at

the closed suitcase on the floor in front of him, feeling lonely. Maybe it was because in the past few months he'd come to accept the townsfolk as friends. Mrs. O'Malley as family. And Penelope as…

He caught the thought and purposely ousted it. He never should have kissed her. Never should have given her false hope for a relationship that could not go anywhere. And he knew she felt it, had seen it glistening in her dark eyes when he'd reluctantly pulled away from her. If he hadn't kissed her, she probably would view his abrupt disappearance much as everyone else would. Mysterious, but nothing to interfere with normal day-to-day life beyond the gossip his actions would generate. But the kiss, well, the kiss had changed all that.

For reasons he couldn't begin to understand, Penelope Moon and her grandmother Mavis lived in some sort of self-imposed exile on the edge of town, just beyond the bridge where he'd met her during his walk earlier. Nearly every day he watched her open her shop…alone…then close it up…alone…nary a person to help break the monotony of a life that so much resembled his own. But where his reasons for keeping everyone at arm's length were clear to him, hers weren't.

For the first time since losing his family, someone had managed to climb into his heart and his head.

And while he knew his leaving would bring her pain, a selfish side of him was glad that she had made him feel something beyond the numbness with which he'd grown so familiar.

And the long months, perhaps years ahead of him would be filled with something in addition to despair.

Hope.

Hope that maybe life could be normal for him again one day.

A soft sound came out of Penelope's mouth. The part sigh, part moan was so unlike any sound she'd ever heard herself make before. The shadow blocking her vision moved, then Aidan was grinning at her, amplifying the sounds around her, sharply contrasting colors, until just merely being alive seemed too much to bear.

She reached out for him, somehow realizing this was a dream and that she was free to do what she would for these precious few moments—

"Get...up!"

Something beneath Penelope's feet trembled. She'd heard of the ground shaking before, but this—

She awakened with a start to realize it wasn't the ground that was shaking beneath her feet as a result of Aidan's kiss, but rather the sheet being yanked from underneath her.

Mavis was staring at her wild-eyed. Penelope

gasped, then watched as the old woman resumed trying to strip her bed while she was still in it.

"Get up, I said!"

Penelope quickly gathered her wits and scrambled to stand on the other side of the narrow bed. The abrupt movement caught her grandmother off guard. She stumbled backward as the bottom sheet easily gave way, nearly knocking her flat on her butt on the hard wood floor.

"Now, what did you go and do that for?"

Penelope reached for her robe, squinting against the sunlight spilling into the room from the window. "Why are you trying to strip my bed while I'm still sleeping at the ungodly hour of..." The face of the electric alarm clock looked black, so she picked up her wristwatch as she shrugged into her robe. "Of nine." Her eyes widened. "Nine?" She stared at her grandmother. "Is it really nine o'clock?"

"What are you asking me for? Does anybody ever really know what time it is?" She cocked her head as she stripped the remainder of the bed linens. "That's a Chicago song, isn't it? I'd get my cassette, but, oh! I threw out all my cassettes."

Penelope stepped into her path, tamping down her anxiety about having overslept and stopping her grandmother from leaving the room with the sheets. "What do you mean, you threw out all your cassettes?"

Mavis squinted her dark eyes. "I don't believe my comment needs explanation."

"And my cassettes?"

Mavis tried to go around her. "You don't have any cassettes." She smiled at her. "Not anymore."

"Mavis!" she shouted, catching the bony woman by the shoulders. "What is the matter with you?"

"Me? What's the matter with me? This from a woman who has never been out on a single date? At least, not any that I know about. And seeing as I know everything about you, I know you haven't been out on a single date."

Penelope opened and closed her mouth a couple of times. "What does that have to do with anything?"

"It has everything to do with everything," Mavis countered. "And, by the way, it's Grandmother. Not Mavis," she said.

Penelope stepped to block her again. "Give me the sheets."

"I will not."

"I said give me the sheets, Grammy."

They stood like that, locked in silent combat, until finally Penelope gave in.

"Okay, then, tell me what you plan to do with them."

"What do you think I plan to do with them?"

Penelope could only imagine.

"I'm going to wash them, of course."

Penelope wished she could believe her. She sighed and stepped aside.

"I'm going to soak them in a mild lye solution, you know, to get rid of any DNA evidence, then I'm going to burn them."

"What!"

Penelope rushed after her, but halfway down the hall Max leapt at her, nearly knocking her down. Oh, God. What was the dog doing in the house? Mavis hated the dog.

Penelope caught Max's mammoth paws in her hands and looked him straight in the eyes. "Now is definitely not the time." She gently released his paws, and he stood there considering her. "Outside."

"Gram, what's Max…?"

Her words trailed off as she realized exactly how Max had gotten into the house. The doors, both the screen and the wood, were missing from their hinges. She marched to the back of the house to find the same there.

She stood, dumbstruck, in the middle of the kitchen, watching through the open doorway as Mavis stuffed the sheets into a large old oil barrel that had been cleaned and filled with water. Wood burned underneath.

She closed her eyes, wondering if she was still dreaming.

No, not dreaming. This would definitely fall solidly into nightmare territory.

She opened her eyes again, but unfortunately everything was as it had been when she closed them.

She looked at the wristwatch still in her hand. She didn't have time for this. She really didn't.

"Gram, you…" she began, standing in the open doorway.

Mavis looked at her as if she were pulling weeds in the garden rather than destroying her bed linens.

"Oh, just forget it. I've got to get to the shop." She slowly pointed her finger at the older woman, then back at herself. "You and me, we're going to have a little talk later."

She turned on her heel and headed back to her bedroom, only to come to a halt at the door. She eyed the piece of wood, relieved to find the hinges were accessible only from the inside. She backtracked to the kitchen, rummaged through the junk drawer for the five or so skeleton keys fastened by a twist tie, then went back to her bedroom and tried each key until she found the one that worked on her door. She wasn't taking any chances. She was going to lock her bedroom lest she come home later and find Mavis had gotten rid of everything that was hers.

"Let her do what she wants to her own stuff," she muttered, checking to make sure her window screen was secure, then slamming and locking the window itself, "but she had better not touch mine."

She turned around and nearly tripped over Max.

"Out!" she yelled.

To her surprise, Max tilted his head, gave a little whine, then turned and left the room, his nails click-clicking against the floor.

Penelope drew a deep breath. If only bringing her grandmother back to reality were so easy....

Chapter Five

That evening at seven, Aidan called the Fourth of July committee meeting to order with a simple holding up of his hand and a clearing of his throat. Seeing as he was the only male in the group, that was about all it usually took. The fifteen women who weren't already seated took their seats inside St. Joseph's gymnasium. Aidan stared down at his notes, giving the others a few moments to settle.

But it wasn't his notes he was thinking about. Rather, he was considering the suitcase that sat packed in his room, the bus schedule in his pocket, and what his life would be like when he left later that night.

That morning he'd decided to tie up some loose ends before he left. At school he'd left his teaching schedule, grading book and other pertinent information on top of his desk so a substitute teacher could easily pick up where he had left off. And if his fifteen summer school students thought his behavior a little odd as he pulled each of them aside to talk to them about their futures, well, they were at the age when they thought the world at large was strange.

He'd written a long note to Mrs. O'Malley, thanking her for her generosity, complimenting her on her impressive culinary skills, and including a passport application and a handful of banknotes for her to take that trip to Ireland she always talked about.

"Is someone in charge of this meeting or not?" Elva Mollenkopf muttered from where she sat at the opposite end of the table.

Aidan blinked and glanced at her.

"Mr. Kendall?" Mrs. Noonan asked from where she sat at his left. "Is everything all right?"

He managed a smile in the direction of the head of the Old Orchard Women's Club. "Fine. Everything's fine." A lie, to be sure. Because he doubted anything ever would be fine in his life again.

"Now, the first order of business is the pink crepe paper that Jeanine has left over from the Valentine's Day Dance...."

And off they went. The heated debate that had

essentially taken up the bulk of time allotted for their meeting two nights ago once again threatened to monopolize the meeting. That was the whole reason they'd had to meet twice in one week, because they'd been unable to accomplish half of what needed to be done at the previous meeting. And Aidan intended to at least make some progress before he left tonight.

He held up his hand again. "I say it's time we vote."

All eyes turned toward him. Usually there was no reason for an official vote. In his experience over the past year, the members of the five or so groups on which he'd sat usually reached agreement. Just another reminder that things were not proceeding as normal in any aspect of his life just now.

He stoically held all of their gazes. "All in favor of going with the pink crepe paper, raise their hands."

Jeanine's hand immediately went up, followed more hesitantly by her best friend Kathy's. Then six more.

Aidan made a note. "Okay, now, all against the pink color then and in favor of red, white and blue crepe paper…"

All the remaining hands shot up before he could finish the question.

"I vote against," he said, then rubbed his thumb

and forefinger against his eyelids. Dead even vote for and against.

Great.

The door on the opposite side of the gym opened, letting in a shaft of late-evening sunlight and making the person who was entering all but impossible to see. Then the metal door clanked shut.

All discussion immediately stopped as everyone turned toward the new arrival.

Penelope.

Aidan's throat tightened as he looked at the woman who had paralyzed his thoughts for the better part of last night and today. She wore a simple powder-blue cotton dress and sandals, her hair pulled back into a long braid.

''What's *she* doing here?'' he heard Elva mutter.

Aidan stilled the woman with a glance. ''I invited her.''

But he hadn't had any idea that she would take him up on it.

He pushed himself from his chair when it looked as if Penelope was having second thoughts and about to turn for the door. ''Miss Moon, welcome. I'm glad you could make it.''

Penelope stood on the polished floor of the basketball court, wondering what in the world she was doing here. She hadn't been inside a school since her own awful memories of high school, and standing here as she was, everyone's eyes on her, made her remember those days all too clearly.

She hadn't even realized that this was where she was heading, until the door had closed behind her and she'd found herself staring at the small gathering across the gym. One minute she'd been at home wrapping up the dinner Mavis had refused to eat, her head pounding from where her grandmother had moved from the dining room into the living room with her hammer, the next she had been tying Max up outside the school.

Aidan stepped across the court to take her arm. The instant his hand made contact with her elbow, the world seemed to shift. She looked into his grinning face and knew exactly what she was doing here. She'd wanted to see him again. Needed to see him again. If only to verify that what had passed between them last night had, indeed, passed between them.

"Why don't you come have a seat?" he said, loud enough for everyone to hear. Then he leaned closer and whispered, "I'm glad you changed your mind."

She followed him to the table, and she began to move toward the only available chair, next to Elva.

But Aidan said, "Here, let me get a chair for you."

He grabbed a metal folding one from a stack and opened it for her, placing it right next to where he'd been sitting.

"Thank you," she said, clearing her throat and gazing into the curious faces of the other women present.

"Everyone, you know Penelope Moon, don't you? I asked her to join us to give the group a fresh perspective."

More like offer up fresh blood for the kill, Penelope thought, scanning the faces of the women and Elva's puckered puss.

"What was that, Elva?" Aidan asked.

"I said, there's nothing wrong with the current perspective."

Aidan's smile never wavered, Penelope noticed, wondering how he did it. How could he tolerate the intolerable woman when she seemed so bent on making everyone's life miserable?

Another woman shifted to Elva's right. "So, let's hear what Miss Moon—"

"Penelope, please," she said.

"Fine. Let's hear what Penelope has in mind for the Fourth of July celebration that none of us has already thought of."

"Jeanine," Aidan said in a low voice.

Penelope reached out and lightly touched his arm. "No, that's all right." Her palm tingled from where it made contact with the springy hair on his forearm. She withdrew it and laid it with the other in her lap. "Actually, I was considering fashioning Lucas Circle after *A Midsummer Night's Dream.*"

Silence met her suggestion.

Aidan appeared surprised.

"Oh, Shakespeare," Mrs. Noonan said, clapping her hands together, the first to break the silence. "I adore Shakespeare."

Penelope looked at Aidan, who was grinning at her.

"I adore Shakespeare, too," he murmured, making her feel as if they were alone. And making her feel that he wasn't really talking about the playwright, but her.

He cleared his throat. "Okay, then. I take it everyone is in agreement in welcoming Penelope to our group?"

Everyone but Elva appeared to agree, but Penelope quickly reached out to stop Aidan. Her intention had never been to join. She'd thought for Aidan's sake that she would stop by for this one meeting, not participate on the planning committee.

"Penelope?" Aidan asked. "Is there something you wanted to say?"

She dropped her gaze and her hand at the same time. Then she lifted her head and smiled. "No. Well, aside from...thank you. I look forward to working with all of you."

Two hours later the sun was setting behind the low buildings of downtown Old Orchard and the meeting had just broken up. Aidan held the door open for Mrs. Noonan and Penelope, the last two to exit the gym. He locked the doors after them, the simple action catching him off guard as he realized it would be his last time doing it. He solemnly pocketed the keys. As soon as he returned to the bed-and-breakfast he would put the keys into an addressed envelope to the school principal, along with his letter of resignation and apology.

"Aidan?" Penelope's soft voice reached out to him from where she had freed Max from the steel bike rack and stood holding his leash. "Is everything all right?"

It was all too easy to fall into the darkness of her eyes, disappear there and forget the world existed. If he needed any evidence of this, he had only to think of the past two hours. From the moment she entered that gym he'd forgotten what lay ahead of him. And thought only of what he would be leaving behind.

Mrs. Noonan took a deep breath. "Well, I guess I'll be running along now." She stepped down the walk, her purse hanging from the crook of her elbow, her arm raised. "Good meeting, Aidan. I'll see you next week for the final one."

He found he couldn't meet her gaze. "Good night, Mrs. N."

She laughed quietly. "Mrs. N. Nobody's called me that in eons," she said absently to herself as she steadily walked away.

He stood there for a moment looking after her,

all too aware that Penelope was next to him, waiting for an answer to her question.

"Shall I walk you home?" he asked.

Her smile, while small and self-conscious, lit up her entire face.

"That's far too much to ask." She tugged on Max's leash when he tried to move away. "But I wouldn't mind your keeping me company part of the way."

He easily took her arm in his, but there was nothing easy about his immediate reaction to her skin rubbing against his. He didn't think he'd ever felt skin so soft. The light scent of lavender teased his senses, making him want to bury his nose in her long, silky dark hair.

They walked in silence for a while, watching as the sky darkened from a light blue to a pregnant purple.

"This reminds me of summers in Rhode Island."

He felt her gaze on his profile. In twelve months he'd never given away his true origins. Until now.

"I thought you were from Oregon," she said softly.

He nodded. "I was raised in Oregon," he lied, hating himself as he did so.

She smiled, her body brushing against his as she leaned slightly closer. "I've never been more than fifty miles outside Old Orchard. Tell me what Rhode Island is like."

Rhode Island. Not Oregon. "Not much to tell, really. Inland, it is a lot like this." He gestured to the neat tree-lined street around them. "Except for the smell of the sea." Always the pungent smell of the sea.

She took a deep breath. "I bet it's beautiful in the fall."

"Yes, it is," he said, but his gaze was glued to her face.

Max barked, then rushed out in front of them, pulling the lead and, by extension, Penelope's hand, jerking her from Aidan's half embrace.

"Max!" she scolded in a hushed tone.

Aidan spotted the cat sitting on the sidewalk some twenty feet in front of them. "He spotted Spot."

Penelope regained control of the overgrown dog, and her smile seemed to reach inside and wrap itself around his heart.

Aidan grinned back. "That sounded odd, didn't it."

"No."

She walked easily beside him, but neither made a move to link arms again. Aidan shoved his hands into the pockets of his Dockers to prevent himself from unconsciously reaching out for her.

"So, you've never been outside Old Orchard?"

She shook her head. "No. Well, not far, anyway. I think everyone here has been up to Toledo for some matter or another."

He squinted at her in the growing darkness as the streetlights switched on. "I can't imagine."

"Have you been to a lot of places?" she asked.

"More than I can count."

"Tell me about them."

He tore his gaze from her face and stared at the sidewalk in front of them. They passed Spot with little fanfare. Max sniffed at the fearless feline, but was held at a safe distance with a firm hand by Penelope. They moved farther down the street, then Aidan turned. Was it him, or was the firehouse cat following them?

"You know, they say Spot is psychic."

Aidan stared at Penelope.

"It's true. For as long as the town's been around, there's been a Spot that's hung around the firehouse—"

She leaned in closer, and he caught another whiff of her subtle scent.

"Some believe it's the same cat."

Aidan chuckled. "You don't buy into it, do you?"

She shrugged. "I'm not as interested in that as I am the rumors that surround her."

"What, that he's drawn to those in need, then disappears when the trouble passes?"

She didn't respond immediately. Aidan turned his head to find her watching him in silent contemplation.

He thought about what he'd just said. And about

Spot's presence, both in her shop the morning before and now.

He cleared his throat. "So, who do you think is the one in need?"

They walked for a ways before she said, "There's a mystery about you, Aidan. The whole town talks about it."

He swallowed hard.

"Well, maybe not the whole town. But Elva certainly lets her thoughts be known that you're an outsider and that you don't share much about yourself."

Funny, then, that he'd shared more about himself in the past ten minutes with her than he had with everyone else put together.

"What would you like to know?" he said, tensing before he finished the sentence.

"Have you ever been married?"

He wasn't sure what he'd expected her to ask, but it wasn't that.

"Yes."

Her eyes widened slightly as the two of them slowed to allow Max to drink from a small puddle caused by the caretaker hosing down the sidewalk in front of the church.

"What happened?"

He glanced down, his hands forming fists in his pockets. "I lost her nearly a year and a half ago."

"I'm...I'm sorry."

Such simple words. Really the only response

when someone shared news of that nature. But the meaning behind hers touched him.

"Thank you."

"Is that why you left Oregon?"

He nodded. "It's one of the reasons I left home, yes."

The boulevard slowly gave way to the two-lane route that led out of town. They walked in the grass to the right of the road, the woods a couple of feet away alive with the sound of crickets and locusts. Here and there lightning bugs relieved the darkness.

"Any children?"

The question was asked so quietly he almost didn't hear it.

He didn't answer for a long time. They passed onto the bridge where he'd met up with her the day before, then over it. "Yes. One. A boy."

He hadn't planned to answer her. But it had been so long since he'd talked to anyone about his son, Joshua, that the name just came out. And the instant it did, the tension coiling in his muscles seemed to ease.

"You lost him along with your wife?" she asked quietly.

He looked at her in the darkness, only then realizing they had stopped outside a once-white picket fence; the small house beyond was quiet and dark. "Yes."

One minute he was trying to make out her beautifully familiar features in the dim light, the next he felt her warm, soft lips against his. A mere whisper of a touch.

"I'm so sorry," she said again.

Aidan's throat threatened to close up even as his physical need for the woman standing a hairbreadth away surged high. "So am I."

Then he was kissing her.

He groaned at the gentle sweetness of her mouth as he threaded his fingers in her hair, tilting her face up so he could better meet her lips. Did she have any idea what he felt for her? How much it meant to him to share what he had with her, without worrying that she would someday hurt him with the information? Could she know how much he wanted her in that one moment? How intensely he longed to caress her bare skin, stroke her slick heat, then bury himself deep inside her?

Her soft gasp told him that she just might.

"Penelope! Is that you and that damn dog of yours?"

Aidan watched Penelope's eyes open wide, her lips freezing against his. She pulled back, putting a hand to her mouth as if caught doing something forbidden.

"Your grandmother?"

She nodded, seemingly incapable of words.

He stood for a moment watching her, waiting for her to invite him in.

Instead, Penelope turned to open the gate and let

Max free from his leash. "Thank you for walking me home."

There was the rustle of clothes nearby. Then a rusty female voice, sounding very close, said, "Oh, good. You brought me the man I asked for."

Chapter Six

Penelope wanted the earth to crack open so she could be swallowed up. She wanted to be somewhere, anywhere other than here.

"Grammy!" she whispered fiercely.

Penelope glanced at Aidan.

"Good evening, Ms. Moon," he said, a tinge of amusement in his voice.

"Don't 'Ms. Moon' me. Get in here and let's have a look."

Penelope watched helplessly and hopelessly as Mavis opened the gate and grabbed Aidan by the front of his nicely starched shirt.

"Grandmother, Aidan was just leaving."

"No, he wasn't." She slid Penelope a glance as she led Aidan to the porch. "He just got here."

"But he's not...I mean, he isn't—"

"What, girl? Spit it out already and be done with it."

"He's not here for you."

Penelope wasn't sure who was more surprised, Mavis or Aidan or herself, as she stumbled into the dark house after them.

It wasn't completely dark. Candles flickered in the dining room, casting an eerie red glow that seemed to warn her away rather than invite her in. Uh-oh. She'd forgotten what state Mavis had been in when she'd left her this morning, then again this afternoon. The doors were still missing. The walls were still covered with photos of her mother. And there was the unmistakable scent of bleach everywhere.

Penelope tried a light switch. Nothing. She bit back the desire to ask her grandmother what had happened to the electricity. Despite everything, she desperately wanted Aidan to think her a normal, everyday woman. Not someone who lived with an eccentric old woman who every twelve months or so took a dive into the deep end.

Mavis snorted. "Well, he has to be here for me, because he certainly couldn't be here for you. You don't need a man. Remember?"

Penelope winced away from her words.

"Come in here and let me have a look at you," she heard her grandmother say.

"Hmm," she heard Mavis hum. "A little on the young side, aren't you?"

Penelope slowly walked over to stand in the doorway to the dining room. She gasped. Both at the change in decor and her grandmother's open perusal of Aidan, whom she'd positioned in front of a stand of candles. The dining table was covered with thick red velvet that seemed to drip over the sides. Candlesticks and candleholders were scattered everywhere, black candles of varying sizes filling the room with the scent of wax and making it even hotter than it had been already.

Penelope wanted to groan. A week ago Aidan would have found a fairly normal scene. Mavis probably would have been in the brightly lit, clean kitchen kneading dough for homemade bread, or reading a book in the living room, or even sitting out on the porch mapping out the stars.

Instead, what he encountered would no doubt confirm every strange thing the townsfolk had ever said about the Moons—and then some.

Mavis circled Aidan. "Young, but you'll do."

"Gram!" Penelope stepped between the two. "Aidan is my guest. Not yours."

The old woman stared at her.

Penelope found herself sputtering. "Well… actually, he's not even a guest. He just…walked me home."

"Of course. Because both you and I know that you don't have any friends."

"And when was the last time you had someone over?" Penelope said without blinking.

She noticed her grandmother flinch. But she couldn't deal with that now. As far as she was concerned, Mavis deserved anything she could fling her way.

She turned quickly to Aidan. But what could she possibly say?

"Can I make you some tea, Aidan?" Mavis asked.

Penelope glanced over her shoulder to find her grandmother stirring something in what looked suspiciously like a cauldron atop a gas camping stove.

She nearly fainted dead out.

The expression of horror that Penelope wore touched Aidan in a way that few things ever had. He wanted to help ease her mind, reassure her that while her grandmother's actions were indeed strange, he'd come across people that unsettled him far more than the thin old woman whose dark eyes sparkled with a humor he doubted her granddaughter saw.

Aidan cleared his throat. "So long as the tea doesn't have a pinch of eye of newt in it, I'm game."

Penelope stared at him as if he'd gone as insane as her grandmother.

"Actually, it's chamomile. Grown in our own garden."

"Then, I'd love some."

Mavis made a strange sound then left the room, leaving the two of them alone.

Aidan's gaze flicked over Penelope's pale face in the warm candlelight. Someone else might have shouted or railed or been rude to the old woman who had caught them both off guard. Or grabbed him by the arm and taken him back outside, slamming the door after them—he glanced in that direction, just now realizing there was no door.

But not Penelope.

He took in the proud way she held her shoulders, as if bracing herself for the worst. But not making any apologies or explanations.

"You don't have to stay, you know," she said quietly.

He squinted at her unblinking comment. "I know," he replied, a shudder rushing through him.

Her soft voice spoke to him on so many levels. No, he didn't have to stay. Not here in this house. Not at the bed-and-breakfast. Not in Old Orchard, period.

But, damn it, he wanted to.

He didn't want to go back to Mrs. O'Malley, collect his suitcase and go to meet the last Greyhound out of town. And a small voice told him he didn't have to.

The revelation was freeing and exciting and frightening all at once.

He cracked a smile. "I like your grandmother."

Penelope seemed doubtful at first. Then she smiled shyly. "She's not usually this bizarre. She's going through one of her episodes."

She gestured vaguely with her hand. "What I meant to say is that every now and again she goes through these odd stretches." She looked down so far, her chin made contact with her chest. "You should have been here two years ago when she set up shop in the front yard advertising for personalized curses and spells."

Aidan reached out a finger and lightly ran it over her cheek, marveling at the smoothness of her skin. "I don't know. I think last year's marijuana-growing incident tops that one."

"You weren't in Old Orchard for that, were you?"

"No. But the story was still big news."

She rolled her eyes. "God. Everyone knew about that?"

"Pretty hard to keep news like that quiet in such a small town."

"I know, but..." She sighed.

She didn't finish her thought. And she didn't

need to. Aidan knew all too well what she was trying to say.

"I bet business picks up at your shop during these...stretches."

Penelope gazed at him for a long time before finally smiling. "You're right. It does." She fingered the bracelet around her wrist. "Just today I could barely deal with all the customers."

"Did they ask about Mavis?"

"They asked why we don't have any doors on the house. I told them we were having them replaced."

His hand was still resting comfortably on her shoulder, his finger almost absently stroking her cheek. God, what he would have given to kiss her in that one moment. But even if her mere existence convinced him to stay in town, no matter how strongly his instincts were telling him to leave, he would have to fight his attraction to the woman before him. Because even if he was wrong about his past catching up with him, he knew that wouldn't always be the case. One day very soon everyone would see him for who he really was. And he thought it only fair that Penelope do that without any false hope that circumstances could be otherwise.

"Here we go," Mavis said, reentering the room with a small tray of mismatched cups.

Penelope gave him a beseeching look. He

chucked her under the chin. "I won't stay long. I promise."

"Actually," she whispered. "I was going to ask you never leave...."

From the moment the words exited her mouth, well into the following day, Penelope couldn't bring herself to believe she'd said what she had to Aidan. As she counted out change for Jolie Conrad, she hoped her cheeks weren't flaming red and that her thoughts weren't transparent.

"Is everything all right, Penelope?"

She stared at the woman she had gone to school with. Jolie had always been kind to her. And unfailingly bought teas and lotions from her once a month. But Penelope had never really felt close to the woman who was now the fire chief of the town. She glanced down to where Jolie held the hand of little Eleanor Johansen. Jolie and her husband Dusty had taken the girl in while her father recovered from massive burns sustained when he'd tried to save his wife and Ellie's mother from their burning house a year and a half ago. She'd heard Elva say something about the now five-year-old being the glue that Jolie and Dusty had needed to paste their lives back together. Secretly Penelope had always known the two would find their way back into each other's arms.

She cleared her throat as she realized Jolie waited for an answer. "I'm fine."

"Spot!" Ellie cried, tugging her hand from Jolie's and chasing the black-and-white cat around the counter.

Jolie looked first at the girl and the feline, then back up at Penelope. "Spot's been hanging out here?"

Penelope made a fuss over closing the register and straightening the jars of cream on the counter. "Not that I've noticed."

Out of the corner of her eye she saw Jolie smile.

"I wondered where the little troublemaker had gotten to now. She comes by the station for a few minutes, then up and disappears. Which means…"

Penelope looked at Jolie. "Which means what?"

Jolie shook her head. "I don't know. It's just that every now and again even I believe the rumors about her." She stepped around the counter to collect the five-year-old. "Come on, Ellie. Say goodbye to Miss Moon so we can go home to make those cookies to take to your daddy."

"How is Mr. Johansen doing?"

Jolie's smile widened. "Better. His latest skin grafts are taking and physical therapy is going well. Ellie and I are trekking up to Toledo for a visit where he's being treated. The doctors say he may be able to come home for good in a couple of months."

Penelope shared her smile. That was, indeed, good news. She already knew that Jolie's husband, Dusty—who had long since turned in his firefighter's hat for a hammer—was overseeing the re-building of the Johansen house. She passed it every day on her walk home.

"See you later, Penelope."

"Hmm. Yes, 'bye! Goodbye, Ellie."

"Goodbye, Miss Moon."

After the pair was out of sight, Penelope rounded the counter and went to stand in front of the windows overlooking Lucas Circle. How familiar everything looked. How reassuring. She'd grown up in this town, but she'd never really taken a good look at it or the people who inhabited it. That she was doing so now...

Spot rubbed against her right ankle and meowed.

Penelope stared down at the restless cat. "What is it, girl? Do you want to go outside?"

She opened the door, expecting the cat to dart out, but instead Spot sat down and stared up at her. *That's odd...*

"Afternoon, Penelope."

She nearly jumped out of her skin as she looked up to find Aidan standing in the open doorway.

Spot got up then and sauntered through the door, both Penelope and Aidan watching her.

"Um, hi," she said, feeling the heat return to her cheeks.

"Was that Jolie I just saw leaving?"

She nodded and turned away from the door, leaving him to catch it and decide whether or not to come in. After last night's debacle and what she'd said, she wasn't sure which she wanted him to do. But she was relieved when the bells sounded as the door closed and he was inside rather than out.

She busied herself with picking up the two boxes that had been delivered earlier and putting them on the counter.

"Beautiful day, isn't it."

She made a face. "Pardon me?"

He gestured toward the windows. "I was just saying it was a nice day. Much too nice to be inside. Especially on a Saturday."

She located the box cutters and opened the first package. "Saturday's when I do my best business."

Actually, the past few days she'd done more business than she had in the entire previous month. This morning, she'd taken in enough to nicely add to the little nest egg she'd been building ever since she'd started working at the shop. Her first profits went straight to the running of the store. Second went to the upkeep on the house she and Mavis shared. The rest, well, the rest she quietly tucked away for a rainy day. Only, she wasn't sure what constituted a rainy day and what she would do with the funds once she figured it out.

Of course, she preferred not to think about the reason behind the pickup in business. It seemed that while she'd been at the planning committee meeting, Mavis had been spotted in town wearing her most hideous housecoat and the fluffy pink slippers Penelope had bought her as a gag gift one Christmas. She'd reportedly been picking through the red and white annuals planted in half-barrels every ten feet or so, and pinching off dead blooms, all the while talking to herself.

"Have you ever taken a vacation, Penelope?"

She blinked at him as if he were speaking a foreign language. "Vacation?"

"Mmm-hmm." He grinned. "You know, as in taking time off, away from the shop."

"Who would pay the electric bill at the house?"

Assuming that someone actually used the electricity at the house. Last night it had taken her a half an hour and a flickering flashlight to discover that Mavis had turned off all the switches in the fuse box. Penelope had turned them all back on, then placed a lock on the fuse box when she was done, hoping that in the morning her electric alarm clock would still be working and would wake her up.

"Everyone needs a little time off," Aidan said quietly.

"Do they?" She sifted through green packing peanuts and took out boxes of Mountain Tea she'd ordered from Greece. "I hadn't noticed."

"Have dinner with me."

Her gaze riveted to his face. "What?"

The little crinkles around his rich brown eyes deepened as he grinned. "I asked if you would do me the pleasure of having dinner with me. Tonight. Take time out from being yourself for just an hour or two.''

''If I'm not myself, who would you be having dinner with?'' she asked, puzzled by his comment, then instantly embarrassed by her question.

''That's what I'm hoping to find out,'' he said quietly.

Her face grew even hotter, if that were possible. She reached over and lowered the temperature on the thermostat, glad for the immediate blast of cold air that hit her from a vent above.

''Name your preference. We could do steak, seafood. I'm even up for a burger and fries at the pub if that's more your style.''

Penelope averted her gaze. Did she even have a style? She'd only been to a restaurant once in her life. And that had been a coffee house-diner with her mother.

She swallowed hard. ''Thank you for the invitation, but I can't.''

''You can't, or won't?''

She didn't answer. Did it matter? It was the same thing, wasn't it? Couldn't, or wouldn't?

He reached across the counter and tipped her face up to force her to look at him.

''Can't, or won't, Penelope?''

Chapter Seven

How he hated the shadow in her tortured dark eyes. But Aidan had to do it. The instant he'd made the decision to ignore his gut and stay in town, he focused on exploring a friendship with Penelope. And part of being a friend meant encouraging the other to do what she normally wouldn't.

"I just can't," she said again.

"Good," he said, dropping his arm to his side. "I'll see you here when you close at five."

"What?"

Aidan merely grinned, winked at her, then casually left the shop, though he felt anything but casual inside.

The truth was, he wasn't sure it was such a wise idea to push Penelope. He didn't know where Penelope's boundaries were. Push too fast, too hard, and she might shut him out, much the same way she shut out everyone but her grandmother.

He remembered last night—the look on her face when she quietly asked him never to leave. He had felt an immediate need to protect her, to help her.

He didn't care what he had to do. Or at what cost. He would help Penelope Moon in a way that he couldn't help himself.

"Sheriff Cole." He nodded at the young man in uniform where he stood in front of the library.

"Afternoon, Aidan."

As Aidan passed by, he felt the hair on the back of his neck stand up. It was a way he'd never felt until the day after the gas station robbery. Was it all in his mind, this suspicion that everyone was looking at him differently? Or could there be a grain of truth to it?

Whatever it was, he'd decided to stay and ride this out to its natural conclusion. In truth, he was tired of running. Tired of packing his suitcase and hitting the road to nowhere. Of being alone, keeping people at arm's length and waiting for the shadow following on his heels to catch up with him and suffocate him. Maybe that was the reason he'd stayed in Old Orchard to begin with. Perhaps he'd subconsciously known that this was the place where his running would end.

For starters, he had to stop running from Penelope Moon and whatever bonds were developing between them.

This wasn't happening. It couldn't be. She, Penelope Moon, was not out on a date with one of Old Orchard's most eligible bachelors at one of Old Orchard's most popular gathering places.

She fiddled with the skirt of her violet cotton dress, wishing she could have gone home to change, taken a bath so that her skin smelled like rose petals, put her hair up. In some way to have done something special to reflect how unique the occasion was.

"Penelope?" Aidan's voice reached for her across the pitted pine table at Eddie's Pub. "Are you all right?"

She blinked up at him, feeling…surreal.

How many times had she passed the pub? And yet she'd never seen the inside, aside from the brief glimpses she got in the summer when Eddie sometimes left the door open. She was vaguely surprised by the pervasive smell of beer. The rugged decor. The familiarity with which the patrons—people she'd known all her life—entered and took stools at the bar. In fact, she and Aidan were two of the few seated at one of the dozen or so tables.

She suddenly realized she hadn't answered Aidan, and laughed nervously. "I'm…fine."

"Are you sure? We could always go somewhere else if you'd like."

"No!" she said a little too quickly, thinking she would only feel more uncomfortable elsewhere. "I mean, here is fine."

In fact, she didn't know what she was doing there at all. Throughout the day she'd resolved to thank Aidan for the invitation to dinner but politely decline. But as she and Maximus stood outside the front door while she locked up, Aidan's smile had been so warm, so handsome, so full of kindness, that she hadn't been able to say anything at all. She'd merely followed when he took her arm and led her across the street to the pub.

There was a bark of laughter at the bar, and Penelope's face grew hot. She chanced a glance to find the McCreary brothers eyeing her and Aidan curiously. Oh, God. She'd known this wasn't a good idea.

The moment they'd walked in the door, she'd been aware of every eye in the place on her. They were all probably wondering what she was doing there. And with Aidan Kendall, no less. She, the odd girl who lived with her crazy grandmother just outside of town, and Aidan, a respectable schoolteacher who could have any single woman he chose.

She gazed deep into his brown eyes. Why *had* he chosen her?

"Because I wanted to," he said quietly.

Had she really said the question aloud?

Penelope opened her eyes wide and pretended an interest in the menu, though she really didn't see a word of it.

"Have you decided?"

"Hmm?"

Aidan gestured toward the menu. "Have you decided what you're going to have yet?"

"Have? Oh." Panic collected in her stomach. "I'm sorry. Am I taking too long? I'm taking too long, aren't I. You probably have things you need to do and I'm holding—"

The feel of his hand on hers nearly sent her catapulting from her sandals. But the instant she saw his smile, she felt all right again. Almost.

"No, Penelope, you're not taking too long. I just wondered if maybe you needed help. A recommendation."

Help. Oh, boy, did she ever need help. But she didn't need it in the form of a dish recommendation. She needed to consult the stars. Mars was hovering overhead, which would explain the chaos swirling inside her. But it was Venus's bright glow that made her heart pound hard.

She offered a small smile, then looked back at the menu, feeling silly but unable to stop herself. "Do you feel like everyone's looking at us?"

What she meant to say was "me." But she was glad she hadn't.

Aidan nodded toward the door. Penelope turned

her head slightly to watch a young man come in. She was surprised to see that every person in the place turned to watch him enter and that there was a heartbeat of a pause before Eddie greeted him and he took a place at the bar.

Was Aidan pointing out that everyone looked at everyone else?

If she'd felt silly before, now she felt doubly so.

As a double Capricorn, she was usually practical about such matters. But the one thing most astrologers didn't emphasize enough was environment. She knew that the tamest Leo could turn into a deadly Scorpio if his or her environment dictated.

As a loner, she tended to internalize things too much. Take them too personally.

And the fact that she may have been doing that all of her life, lending a self-absorbed slant to her usually positive traits, well, surprised and bothered her.

Aidan leaned closer. "If they are giving you a little extra attention, it's because you're beautiful to look at."

Penelope's cheeks flamed for an entirely different reason, but she tried to shrug off the compliment. "Pisces."

His brows drew slightly together, then realization dawned and he grinned. "Nope."

She sighed heavily and lay her menu down. "Are you ever going to tell me what your sun sign is?"

An odd expression passed over his face, then was gone. "No."

"Why not?"

"Because if I do, you'll pigeonhole me. You'll use those charts to try to piece me together like some assembly-required toy."

"Scorpio."

His deep chuckle made her squeeze her thighs together.

A woman standing next to their table cleared her throat. Penelope's smile instantly disappeared. Were they going to be asked to leave?

"Hi, Frannie," Aidan said easily. "Any specials for tonight?"

She was the waitress.

Penelope wanted to crawl under the table. If only the move would allow her to escape herself.

The young woman wearing a blue T-shirt with the pub's name across her chest took a pad out of her back pocket. "We have beer-batter shrimp and some lake perch we got fresh this morning."

"Sounds good."

"You're Penelope Moon, aren't you?" the waitress asked.

Penelope blinked up into her face. "Yes. Yes, I am."

She smiled. "I'm Jeanie. I've heard great things about your shop. I keep meaning to come by and get a better look inside."

"You should," Aidan said, when Penelope couldn't think of a response.

"I think I will."

She looked at Penelope expectantly.

"Would you like me to order for both of us?" Aidan asked.

Penelope could feel her body deflate as she exhaled the breath she was holding. "Yes. Yes, please."

Aidan handed Jeanie his menu. "I'll have the perch, and why don't you bring Penelope the shrimp? Oh, and bring us a plate of those fried onions Chef makes so well."

"Will do."

Jeanie left their table, slid the menus next to the cash register and disappeared into the kitchen.

Penelope picked up her glass of cola and sipped it.

"So tell me," Aidan said, relaxing back into his wood chair. "What is your sign?"

Penelope raised her brows. "What?"

He crossed his arms and shrugged. "Well, I figure since you keep asking me about mine that you think yours reveals something about you."

Maybe a little too much, Penelope thought. "Capricorn."

"The goat, right?"

She smiled. "Yes, the goat."

"Does that mean you're stubborn?"

She nearly sprayed the table with her cola. "You're thinking of Taurus."

"No, I'm thinking of Capricorn."

"Do you know anything about astrology?"

"I know about astronomy. And the stories associated with the constellations." His smile widened. "And I also happen to have been around goats, and they can be just as stubborn as bulls, just smaller."

Aidan watched Penelope blush prettily. He didn't know many women past the age of eighteen who blushed anymore. Either they had already heard and seen it all, or they didn't know how to take a compliment. And while Penelope never openly accepted or voiced appreciation for compliments, she was obviously touched by them. And touching her on an emotional level made him want to touch her on a physical one.

Would the skin of her stomach flush when he bared it to the night air? Would she shiver if he licked the supple expanse, then blew on it? Would she bite her bottom lip as she tried to keep from calling out, then ultimately give herself over to his attentions and her own emotions?

Would there ever come a time when he might freely pursue the answer to those questions?

Someone came to the door of the pub and said something to those inside. There was much screeching as stools were pushed back and a few patrons moved to the open doorway.

"Were you always a teacher?" Penelope asked him quietly, completely unaware of the activity behind her.

Aidan moved his napkin and silverware farther to the left, then rested his hands on the table. "No."

She watched him as if waiting for him to offer more. When he didn't, she dropped her gaze to his hands.

"I'm sorry. That was too forward, wasn't it."

So confident in so many ways, it was surprising that she lacked confidence when it came to relationships. "Penelope, asking someone if they have herpes is forward. Asking what another person does for a living isn't."

Of course, having said that, he'd cast himself in a suspicious light for not easily sharing his past.

"I used to work in construction."

"Construction?"

He nodded. "Yes, you know, doing small carpentry jobs. Adding built-in bookcases. Crown molding. Wainscoting. Things like that."

"Doesn't sound small to me."

"No, but I wasn't exactly building houses, either."

"Do you know how to install doors?"

He chuckled quietly. "What's to say Mavis won't just take them off again?"

She sighed and relaxed slightly in her chair. "I moved everything that I couldn't bear the thought of losing to my bedroom and I lock the door every night. But I'm afraid she's going to either pick the lock or gain access through the window and I'm going to go home to find everything gone."

She said this as if Mavis's behavior were par for the course. And maybe for her, it was. Having met and spent a little time around Mavis the other night, he admitted to thinking the older woman wasn't the unbalanced senior she portrayed. Rather, she seemed to map out each of her peculiar doings as if hoping to provoke a reaction. But what kind of reaction? And why?

"Have you ever thought about getting your own place?" Aidan asked.

Penelope stared at him. "You mean, leave my grandmother?" She shook her head. "No. Never."

"Why not?"

This appeared to stump her.

Aidan didn't think it was an unusual question. Eventually everyone came to a point when they wanted to strike out on their own. Claim their own space. But it was apparent the thought had never even occurred to Penelope.

"Why not indeed…" she said quietly, a curious light in her eyes.

"Aidan and Miss Moon?" Eddie called from the door. "You two, um, might want to come have a look at this."

Penelope's soft brows drew together. Aidan considered telling the bar owner they were otherwise occupied.

"Max," Penelope whispered.

Aidan pushed back from his chair and followed as she hurried for the door.

At first it wasn't apparent what everyone was looking at. What was clear was that nearly everyone within shouting distance was standing outside, staring at something going ón in Lucas Circle. Aidan squinted, trying to get a better look, but there were too many people blocking his view.

He watched Penelope crouch down and pet Maximus where he was straining against his leash near the light pole, barking at the area of interest.

"Come on in! The water's fine!" a woman called.

Penelope jumped up and an expression of horror crossed her face. He lightly grasped her hand as she pushed her way through the throng of people, then came to a jarring stop.

Aidan moved to her side, staring at what everyone else saw. Namely, her grandmother, in nothing but her underwear, splashing in the fountain in the middle of Lucas Circle. And she was reaching for the back of her bra as if to undo it....

Chapter Eight

Penelope couldn't believe this was happening...again. As she signed the form accepting responsibility for her grandmother and paying a fine that made an ugly dent in her savings, she wished not only that she didn't live with Mavis, but also that she lived far, far away. Someplace, anyplace, that wasn't here.

Sheriff Parker scratched the top of his handsome head and grinned sheepishly. "You've got to make it clear to your grandmother that she can't be doing stuff like that out in public, Penelope."

Like she had control over what her grandmother

did or didn't do. She only wished she could some-how intuit the old woman's intentions so she could at least make sure she wasn't anywhere around when her grandmother put on a show.

Cole motioned toward Desk Sergeant George Johnson, who went to the back of the office, ap-parently to bring Mavis out.

She eyed Aidan where he stood outside, Max's leash in his hand, staring at Lucas Circle as if he'd never quite look at it the same way again.

"You know," the sheriff was saying, "you may want to arrange another visit with a doctor for her."

They both knew he wasn't talking about a med-ical doctor. And they both also knew that it wouldn't do a lick of good. After last year's de-bacle with the medical marijuana, the court had ordered psychological counseling. And after three appointments, the young female psychologist had called Penelope at the shop to tell her she couldn't see Mavis anymore. She not only didn't think she was helping her, but also was afraid Mavis might ultimately affect the counselor's own grip on san-ity.

Penelope had understood.

By the time that had all transpired, summer had passed and her grandmother had gone back to nor-mal.

Well, as normal as her grandmother got, anyway.

"I'll see what I can do, Sheriff," she said, smiling nervously.

She heard Mavis before she saw her. "What's the matter with all of you? Never seen a human body before? The human form is beautiful. Nothing at all to be ashamed of."

They reached the front room and Mavis looked at Penelope, then the sheriff. "You should know better than to question the request of the king."

"The king?" Sheriff Cole repeated, clearing his throat.

"The king of all rock and roll. The man in the big pink Cadillac in the sky."

Elvis? Was Mavis saying she was taking orders from Elvis? No, it couldn't be.

Penelope quickly stepped forward, putting her arm over her grandmother's robe-covered shoulders. "Thank you, Sheriff. I'll make sure Dottie gets her robe back, washed, first thing tomorrow."

"No problem, Penelope. Just you, um, remember what we talked about."

"I will." She would do one better than that. When they got back to the house, rather than locking her bedroom door, she was going to lock Mavis in her own room. Board up the windows. Anything to keep her from flashing the good folks of Old Orchard again.

They stepped outside, and Aidan turned to face them.

"Oh, it's you. Good," Mavis said, taking his

arm and heading in the opposite direction of home.
"Couldn't stay away from me, now, could you?"

Penelope sighed in exasperation, grasped her
grandmother's arm and coaxed her in the right direction. "Home is this way."

Mavis did another about-face, taking Aidan with
her. He met Penelope's gaze over her grandmother's gray head.

"The truck's over this way."

"The truck? You drove the truck into town?"

She hadn't even been aware the old Ford still
ran. It had been shut up in the garage for the past
five years, neither her grandmother nor her driving
it. Penelope didn't have the need. The shop was
within walking distance, no matter the weather.
And Mavis…well, Mavis usually stuck close to the
house.

She only wished that applied all the time.

"I think we should walk," Penelope said.

"I agree," Aidan said.

"What about the truck?"

Penelope looked at Aidan. He cleared his throat.
"I'll bring it by the house tomorrow morning."

"Tomorrow morning's too late. I have things I
need to do tonight."

"Tonight? What do you have to do tonight?"
Penelope asked. "No. Scratch that. You're not doing anything tonight."

"Are you disobeying the king, as well?"

The king? Aidan mouthed over Mavis's head.

She rolled her eyes and mouthed, *Don't ask.*

"I'll bring it by tonight," Aidan promised.

Mavis's step seemed to grow lighter. "Good."

"But that doesn't mean you're going anywhere in it," Penelope pointed out.

"We'll see…"

Her grandmother was channeling Elvis, her house had no doors, and she was now an even bigger laughingstock in town.

A couple of hours later, Penelope sat on her bed staring at the myriad objects crammed into her bedroom. It was difficult to navigate through the maze of sideboard, armchairs, lamps and boxes. Last night she'd nearly maimed herself when she'd gone on a bathroom run. Forget that having to unlock and then re-lock her bedroom door after herself—a roll of toilet paper in hand in case Mavis decided she had something against the stuff—had completely woken her so that it had been nearly impossible to get back to sleep afterward.

Of course, she wasn't about to admit that Aidan's gentle eyes and charming grin had anything to do with her insomnia….

She glanced at her watch. Just after eleven p.m. She pushed off the bed, took the key from the leather tie around her neck and let herself out of her bedroom, locking up after herself. The house was quiet. Too quiet.

She padded down the hall, now devoid of the

throw rugs she had rolled up and stowed in her room until her grandmother's latest spell passed.

"Gram?" she called out, her plain cotton nightgown swirling around her legs. She tapped on Mavis's door and received no answer. "Gram?" she said quietly, turning the knob and pushing the barrier slightly inward. The new moon shone brightly through the curtainless window, clearly illuminating the empty bed, stripped of linens.

Oh, God.

Last night, she hadn't gone to her room until Mavis promised that she would stay put until morning. She was also glad that she'd asked Aidan not to bring the truck back until late. Late enough to circumvent any strange commands her grandmother thought she was hearing.

She hurried through the house, checking both open doorways. No sign of Mavis.

She rested her fingers against her neck and swallowed hard. She needed a phone.

She went in search of an extension that she could try to hook up to the frayed wires sticking out from the wall. Just then, a vehicle's headlights drifted across the wall, and she heard the unmistakable roar of the old 1962 Ford in the driveway.

Aidan.

She hurried to the front doorway and stood there, her arms wrapped around her upper body, and tried to ignore the anticipatory hammering of her heart.

* * *

Aidan stared at the apparition on the front porch of the old house, half afraid he was seeing things. But time and several blinks of his eyes told him he wasn't. Penelope stood wearing a white nightgown that was nearly transparent under the bright beams of the truck, her lush body clearly outlined under the thin cotton. Her black hair and eyes seemed to glisten; her legs were long and her ankles impossibly slender, her feet free of any toenail polish and downright sexy.

He switched off the engine, leaving the key in the ignition. He'd never thought of someone's feet as being sexy before. And the idea was more than a little disconcerting.

He climbed from the truck, snatching the bag that had been next to him on the bench seat. It seemed to take forever to open the gate and cross over the sidewalk to the porch; all the while, Penelope stayed right where she was, watching him.

He stopped at the foot of the stairs, words eluding him.

"It seems Mavis didn't need the truck, after all," Penelope said, her words soft on the night air.

Aidan squinted at her. "She's gone?"

Penelope sighed and nodded. "Who are we to question the king's bidding?"

Aidan still wasn't entirely sure who "the king" was or why he was telling Penelope's grandmother to do odd stuff, and he wasn't all that sure he wanted to find out, either.

He held out the plain white paper sack. "I brought the food we weren't able to eat earlier."

Her eyes grew so round, he was afraid he'd done something wrong.

"You've eaten already," he said simply.

"No. I'm just surprised not only that I haven't eaten, but that I completely forgot about...well, dinner."

"Well, I guess I'm just in time, then."

"For what?"

"To save you from starving to death."

They stood there for a long time, nothing but the sound of crickets and the light of the sliver of moon and lightning bugs. Max lay on the far side of the porch, having barely lifted his head when Aidan pulled into the drive. His eyelids were already drooping back down.

"So..." Aidan said. The night was thick with expectation. And knowing that the two of them were out there alone, Penelope in her nearly sheer nightgown, he didn't think it a good idea to tempt fate. He already wanted this woman far more than was wise. "I guess I should be going."

He handed her the bag, the sound of the paper crumpling overly loud in the quiet night.

"Good night," he said, hoping the long walk back to the bed-and-breakfast would be enough to get his runaway thoughts and traitorous body under control.

"Good night," she whispered.

He turned and began walking toward the gate.

"Aidan?"

He stopped but didn't dare turn around.

"Please stay."

There wasn't a single man alive who could resist such an invitation.

Aidan knew he should. He stood stock-still for several moments, his hands deep in the pockets of his pants, his back stiff, his breathing shallow. Then his body turned back toward the woman standing at the top of the steps, the bottom of her nightgown shifting in the wind.

She didn't say anything. She merely led the way through the doorless doorway. But rather than leading him to the kitchen as he'd expected she would, she led him down a dark hall. He heard the jingle of keys, then she reached out and took his hand and led him into a room filled with starlight shining through wispy white sheers.

As Aidan's eyesight adjusted, he realized they were in her bedroom.

She put the bag of food down on top of something he couldn't make out, locked the door, then turned to face him. The thump-thump of his heart was so loud, he was surprised she couldn't hear it. She slowly reached down, fingered the hem of her nightgown, then pulled the light cotton over her head, revealing that she wasn't wearing anything underneath.

A metal band seemed to squeeze around Aidan's chest as he watched her drop the nightgown so it pooled in a white puddle at their feet. Then she squared her shoulders, bravely baring all to him.

Oh, hell…

Oh, heaven…

A lump lodged in his throat as he drank her in. Her hair was a dark tangle around her pale face and smooth shoulders, running down to almost cover her small but perfectly proportioned breasts. The soft mounds stood as proudly as she did, her pale nipples engorged, moving as she took deep, ragged breaths. His hungry gaze slid down to her impossibly narrow waist, her abdomen flat, her navel bearing a navel ring. He reached out to touch the little hoop of silver, fascinated by her quick intake of breath as the backs of his fingers brushed against her lower belly. He slowly drew his hand back and allowed his gaze to continue caressing her past the surprising piece of body jewelry to the wedge of springy dark curls at the apex of her thighs, then to the lush flare of her hips and long, long legs to her feet. The sweet scent of rose petals and her own unique musk filled his senses, making him close his eyes and breath it in.

"Aidan?" she said, her voice as insubstantial as the thin curtain fluttering in the light summer breeze. "Please touch me."

He let out a groan. *I can't,* he wanted to tell her. *I shouldn't,* he wanted to say. But instead he slowly reached his hand out, snaking it around her elegant neck and under the heavy fall of her hair. He leaned forward and brushed his lips against hers, then leaned his head the other way and gave them another pass. Then he was kissing her so deeply, he swore he could count her heartbeats, his tongue swirling, inviting hers out to play. Tentatively she touched the ridge of his teeth with the tip of her tongue and boldly thrust it deep into his mouth. Had he ever experienced anything so devastatingly sweet? So hotly erotic?

Before he knew it, he had swept her up into his arms and carried her to the narrow twin bed across the room, avoiding the obstacles of furniture and boxes. The box springs gave a low *squeak* as he settled her down, carefully placing her head on the pillow. She looked like an angel gazing up at him. And if he knew what was good for him, he would place a kiss on the tip of her nose and say goodnight.

She reached out a shaking hand, touching the hard plane of his stomach through his T-shirt as he stood straight beside the bed. Air whooshed from his lungs, then rushed back in when she tugged the cotton from his jeans and hesitantly pressed her fingertips to his burning flesh.

For a moment he gave himself over to the need to just feel. To allow the sensation of Penelope branding him with her touch to ripple through him, tightening his muscles, heating his blood.

It had been so very long since he'd listened to the needs of his body. Heeded the call of his heart. And even though he knew how dangerous it was to do so now, he couldn't help himself. He craved these few moments, no matter how selfish the desire.

Penelope slid her hand farther up until her palm rasped over his flat nipple. Slowly, he pulled the T-shirt up over his head, dropped it to the floor, then unsnapped his jeans and allowed them to follow, until he stood next to her as naked as she was.

Her eyes widened, and he watched a swallow work its way down her throat as her gaze traveled over him in much the same way his had over her mere moments ago. From his face, over his shoulders, his flat nipples, down over his abdomen. Her soft gasp as she saw the evidence of his arousal set off a quiet warning in the back of his head. But he couldn't listen to it just then.

She pressed her hot palm against his stomach, then slowly started sliding it lower. His breath hissed through his teeth. He closed his eyes, tensing for the moment when she would make contact with his straining erection. There was a feathery touch down the front of the shaft, then her fingers encircled him, squeezing carefully.

He caught her hand in his, then drew it to his mouth to kiss it. He climbed into bed next to her, taking extra care not to catapult either one of them off the narrow mattress. Penelope shifted to her side to make more room, putting them face-to-face. Aidan marveled at her, unable to remember when he'd wanted to make love to a woman more. They touched nowhere, but he felt her presence everywhere. He smoothed her hair back from her face and gently kissed her, then kissed her again. When she was breathless with want, he slid his hand down her clearly defined collarbone to cup her right breast. She shuddered and scooted closer until her womanhood rested against his manhood.

Aidan slowly caressed her, rubbing his thumb over her distended nipple. Then he bent to run his tongue along the enticing bit of flesh, suckling gently. Her back arched in automatic response, her rapid breathing nearly tugging her nipple from his mouth with every intake. The fire that had ignited low in his belly the moment she pulled her nightgown off flared brightly. She was so damn responsive. So trusting. So…open.

He moved his fingers lower, not stopping until they rested at the nest of damp curls between her legs. Where her breathing had been erratic before, now it seemed to stop altogether. He tunneled his fingers into the springy hair, marveling at the way she parted her thighs to him, inviting him closer. It was an invitation he was loath to ignore.

The tip of his index finger found the silken bud of flesh. The narrow bed seemed to shake with her trembling body. He'd forgotten how special it was to be wanted...to be needed.

He slid his finger down until it rested against her slick portal. Slowly he breached the swollen entrance, finding her very, very hot. And very, very tight. Her trembling increased.

"Penelope?" he whispered, burying his face in her fresh-smelling hair. "You aren't...I mean you have..." He wanted to groan. "Have you made love before?"

He didn't hear her answer. Didn't need to. He already knew.

The beautiful woman in his arms was a virgin.

He pulled back to gaze into her face, and saw her desire.

"I want this," she whispered.

Aidan knew what he should do—pull away. He didn't deserve this precious gift. Didn't deserve Penelope Moon and what she was offering him.

He cupped her face in his hand. "Are you sure?" he rasped.

She nodded. "I've never been more sure of anything in my life."

Aidan groaned, pressing his face against her neck, feeling her strong pulse there, tasting the subtle salt of her skin.

He felt her move, then gasped when her fingers encircled his erection.

"Please," she whispered, kissing his shoulder.

"I want you, Aidan. I want you more than any man I've ever met."

And, damn it, he wanted her.

He gently pushed her to lie flat on the mattress, watching as she parted her thighs to him, willingly offering herself up in a way that was painfully sweet and humbling.

He positioned himself against her, then found her bud with his free hand, rubbing her until she was gasping for air.

"Oh, Aidan, please…"

He slowly entered her, encountering the telltale resistance, then pushing through until he slid into her to the hilt. Penelope's back came up off the bed and she froze, her muscles contracting tightly around him at the sharp pain. Aidan lay still for several moments, waiting for the hurt to subside. He moved his hand first. Over her right breast, caressing her with great care, then her left breast, following with his mouth, laving her with his tongue even as they were tightly connected. He drew back and dragged his palm down the middle of her stomach until it pressed against the wedge of dark hair. He parted her swollen folds until he found what he was looking for, then gently stroked her hot flesh.

She began to wriggle. He slowly withdrew, watching her eyes, watching her face, searching for signs that she was ready to continue. Then he slowly reentered her. She moaned, seemingly unable to catch her breath; then her sweet body was moving up to meet his.

He wasn't sure how long it took. Maybe minutes. Maybe an hour. But he gritted his teeth and paced himself, waiting until he felt her muscles constrict in pleasure and not pain, before he allowed himself release, filling her with evidence of his want, his need for her.

Rushing through his mind were two thoughts. That he didn't feel he deserved her. And that he was so damn grateful that she felt differently that it hurt even to breathe.

Chapter Nine

The following morning at the shop, Penelope pored over the real estate section of the *Old Orchard Chronicle* that she had picked up at the General Store. If her state of awareness before last night had been on high, now her body practically thrummed with the knowledge of how things could be between a man and a woman. How things were between her and Aidan.

She shivered, but it had nothing to do with the cool air blowing on her from the vent above. If anything, her skin was flushed, her body temperature high. He had been so gentle. So intuitive. So passionate. He'd turned her inside out with the myriad sensations he'd introduced her to, stroking her, caressing her, both with his hands and his body, until she was out of her mind with pleasure. And with love for the man who had awakened a part of her she hadn't even known existed.

Love...

Such a simple word. But one she hadn't known the true meaning of until now. Until Aidan.

But where could it lead?

Her gaze caught and held on a house listing. The old Jenkins place on the north end of town. She drew a circle around it several times, then stuck the end of the pen into her mouth. Hadn't something happened there recently? Yes. Last year ex-Sheriff John Sparks had caught two fugitives at the abandoned house. It seemed the townsfolk hadn't been the only ones to hear the rumors about Violet Jenkins and the unaccounted-for monies from her late husband's insurance check. When she died, the house had become a magnet for local treasure-hunting teens...and for the two fugitives who shot Darby Parker Conrad—now Sparks—before John caught them and put them away for good.

She stared off into space. If she recalled correctly, the house was a one-story structure much like her and Mavis's place, except that it had been well maintained and sat on a large piece of land that had at one time been a farm. She heard a sigh and, with a start, realized it was her own.

Maximus whined from where he lay at her feet

watching Spot give herself a tongue bath on a chair in the corner.

"What do you think, Max? Plenty of room for you to run around."

The dog looked at her with watery eyes, his tail thumping against the floor.

She eyed the price of the house, her stomach dropping. There was no way she could afford that. Sure, she could make the down payment, but what would the monthly payments be? She couldn't really count on a steady income from the shop.

Moreover, how would Mavis react if Penelope moved out of the house? Who would be around to look after her grandmother when she went through one of her spells?

She sighed again, the sound full of worry rather than wistfulness.

Aidan had left her at about three in the morning. At about four, she'd heard her grandmother return. And when she got up at seven, she found Mavis pulling young plants willy-nilly out of the back garden. Penelope had merely shook her head and absently eaten a bagel that Mavis must have missed in her frenzy to throw everything away.

"I see Aidan brought the truck back," her grandmother had said, not even looking at her.

Penelope had nearly choked on the bagel. She nodded, then told Mavis she was leaving for the shop.

* * *

The bells on the shop door rang, announcing that she had company. She began to throw the newspaper away, then instead tucked it under the counter and watched as Sara Burnham walked in.

"Am I the first?" Sara asked after she said hello.

Penelope smiled. It was Sunday and she didn't open the doors until ten. There really wasn't much reason to open them earlier. Even if she had been there since eight.

"You're the first."

"Good." Sara moved over to the display of experimental scented wax melts in the shape of chocolate bars that Penelope had made at home a few months ago.

Penelope absently watched her. Sara had been a grade under her in school and had always been nice. Her blond hair was always pulled back into a ponytail or French braid. In fact, Penelope couldn't remember a time when she'd seen Sara with her hair down.

Sara gathered up nearly the entire stock of melts and piled them on the counter, her fair skin flushed. "Do you have a basket or something I could use to get more?"

Penelope raised her brows. "Sure." She handed her a wicker basket that was more for show than utility. Truth was, she rarely sold more than a person could hold in her arms.

She quietly cleared her throat as Sara moved

back to the pile. "Is there something I can help you with?"

Sara glanced at her. "What? Oh. I'm sorry." She smiled widely. "It's just that I sent my friend Ginny a gift basket for her birthday and she loved these wax things. Wanted me to send her a dozen of each."

"That many?"

Sara nodded. "You know, they don't have these anywhere else. Ginny says she hasn't seen them in California. I mean, they have those individual flower-looking things, but nothing like these. It's so convenient to just break off a chunk and put it into a diffuser." Her gaze fell on a diffuser that had just come in from India the week before. "Is that new? Oh, it is, isn't it?" She added it to the basket. "I'll take that, as well. For me." She finished filling the basket and moved back to the counter. "You know, you could make a killing on the Internet selling this stuff."

"The wax melts?"

Sara nodded as she helped Penelope unload the bars. "That and the other homemade things you offer. Your hand-milled soap is amazing. Even my fiancé told me I smelled like roses. And I didn't even know he knew from roses."

Penelope shook her head. "Well, I don't know much about the Internet."

Sara waved her hand. "They offer courses at the

community college. Within a month you'd be up and running.''

Penelope laughed as she rang up the order. ''I doubt it. I may do well when it comes to this kind of thing, but me and machines? We don't get along very well. It took me forever to learn how to operate this—'' She indicated the register, which seemed to take its cue and jammed up on her. She met the other woman's gaze, and they both laughed. She cleared the tape and started again from the beginning. ''You know, since you're buying so many at once, I can give you a discount. How does fifteen percent sound?''

''Fantastic! At that price, I just may come and buy up everything you've got and sell it on the corner myself.''

After Sara left, Penelope stood behind the counter, staring at the small pile of wax melts that remained. Could it really be that easy to learn how to operate a computer? She'd seen a bank of them at the library and had even stopped to try to look up a book on her own one time, but she'd given up when the screen made a series of strange beeping noises and went blank.

The bells rang again and she glanced up to find Aidan standing just inside the door, the look in his eyes making her flush from head to toe. But rather than try to hide it, she held her head high.

She was still astounded that she had been so bold as to lead him to her bedroom and strip off her nightgown right there in front of him. But she had known such a wanting, such an acute awareness of him on every level, that her actions had come naturally.

And when he had touched her...

She shivered again, her body tingling. She quietly cleared her throat, waiting for him to say something.

He didn't speak, so she asked, "What do you know about computers?"

Aidan might have expected Penelope to say many things, but "what do you know about computers" definitely wasn't one of them. And now, five hours later, as they headed out to the old Jenkins place in Mavis's rusty truck, he couldn't help but wonder what she had in mind.

It was late Sunday afternoon, and Penelope had closed the doors to her shop early and asked if he would drive her out to the house. He had been surprised by her request, especially when she refused to offer up why she wanted to go, but any excuse to be with her was a good one. He squinted at her in the slanting sunlight. She didn't buy into all the rumors surrounding the place, did she?

"There," she said, pointing to a spot to the right. "Pull into the driveway."

He downshifted with some effort, flicked on the blinker although there was no one else on the two-lane rural road, and pulled into the gravel driveway that ran a ways before coming to a stop next to the Jenkins place.

"Stop here."

They were halfway up the drive to the house. Aidan silently questioned the move, but did as she asked.

Damn, but she was beautiful. The sunlight bounced off her shiny black hair, and her dark eyes were alive as she looked over the small structure twenty yards or so ahead of them. She blindly reached for the door handle and gave a yank; the door opened with a loud groan. She slid down to stand outside, her gaze glued to the house.

Aidan shook his head and switched off the engine, then got out on his side of the truck.

"It's pretty, isn't it," she asked quietly.

The smell of freshly cut grass filled Aidan's nose as he looked over the manicured lawn. Likely the realtor's office saw to the upkeep of the place. It almost looked as if Violet Jenkins still lived there.

Penelope slowly stepped up the drive, stopping every couple of feet or so as if seeing something the previous vantage point hadn't allowed. Aidan followed her gaze. The simple house was in good shape, the black roof was new, the cream-colored vinyl siding and white trim neat. There were curtains at the windows, and he suspected the place probably still held the Jenkins' furniture.

"It's too far to walk to town, isn't it?" Penelope asked.

He looked at her. "Pardon me?"

She looked behind them toward the truck. "I'd have to get a car. Something trustworthy."

"A car?" Aidan tried to make sense out of her words.

Penelope reached out and rested her hand against the white mailbox with hummingbirds and morning glories painted on the side—for show, because the true mailbox sat at the edge of the road.

Then it dawned on him. Penelope was thinking of buying the place.

His legs froze beneath him.

Her asking him to take her there… Her wide-eyed wonder as she took in the place… Her odd comments…

Why hadn't he caught on?

Perhaps because he hadn't wanted to.

He ran his hand slowly through his hair, turning from the house and from Penelope and squinting into the sun. He pretended to consider the surrounding farmland. Well, what had he expected? That she would be the same woman she'd always been? Wasn't he the one who had pressed her to get out, to participate more in the community? He'd even asked if she had ever considered moving from Mavis's house.

Then last night he'd forgotten who he was. He'd given in to his desire for her, accepted the special gift she'd offered up and tried to give back as much as he could.

And for a short stretch of time he had wanted to make himself deserving of that gift. Of her love. Pushing aside that he never would be.

"Aidan?"

He stiffened his shoulders, refusing to look at her. Because when he did he got himself—and now her—into all kinds of trouble.

She stood next to him, gazing out at the landscape.

"It would need more trees," she said. "I could plant a row up the property line here...and over there. Then maybe a stand out back. A few fruit trees, maybe. Pears, cherries, apples."

Aidan clenched his teeth as she fell silent again.

It was only natural that she would want more. Want to live like a normal woman. Have the same dreams other women had. He hadn't thought...

He hadn't thought, period. That was the problem. Sure, he'd considered the impact of getting involved with her. But it had been her uniqueness, the fact that she wasn't like other women, that had caught him off guard. Drawn him in a way no other woman had—his late wife included.

His gut clenched. It was the first time he'd thought of Kathleen in those terms. In the past fourteen months she had remained his wife. Not his *late wife*. Not the woman who had been ripped from his life in a way that had nearly destroyed him. Not the woman he would never see again.

He felt Penelope's light touch on his arm. "Aidan, are you all right?"

His chaotic emotions collided with her tenderness and nearly sent him mentally careening over the edge.

"Fine. I'm fine." He looked at her, purposely keeping his face blank. "Are you ready to head back into town? I have some things I need to do."

The shadow of pain in her eyes was obvious as she hesitantly took her hand back.

"Sure."

Later that night, the sun but a smear of color on the horizon, Penelope sat on the front porch alone, trying to squelch the odd sensation that things had changed between her and Aidan.

She swallowed hard and reached for another sheet of the fluorescent purple tissue paper that she was fashioning into makeshift stars. They would be hung along with white lights from the trees along Lucas Circle for the Midsummer Night's Dream celebration. She finished with the ten-inch-round ruffled star, then attached several stretches of clear piping to the core and tied smaller stars to the ends. She'd worked mindlessly for the past two hours straight and had nearly used up the supplies she'd picked up from Mrs. Noonan the day before. Now she was trying not to think about Aidan and where he was at this moment and what, exactly, had made him so distant from her at the Jenkins house.

A rustling came from the direction of the bushes on the east side of the house. She glanced that way, then at Max, who lay asleep on the opposite side of the porch, Spot curled up next to him.

Another sound. She looked that way again. A small animal? Probably. But that didn't explain the way her scalp itched as if someone were watching her.

A crash sounded from inside the house.

"Gram?" she called.

There was no answer but for several carefully chosen curse words.

Penelope put the completed star down next to the others and got up from the swing. Through the open doorway she watched Mavis crouching to sweep up glass from a broken picture frame. Then, suddenly, it all appeared to be too much for her, and she stopped, falling back from her crouched position to land on her bottom. Penelope watched helplessly as her grandmother's shoulders shook and a deep sob seemed ripped from her very chest.

Penelope went to her instantly and knelt on the floor next to her. "What? What is it? What's the matter?"

The Moon family had never been particularly demonstrative. Oh, sure, they could help you interpret your dreams and choose you a good mate based on your chart, but ask them for a casual hug

The Silhouette Reader Service™—Here's How It Works:

Accepting your 2 free books and gift places you under no obligation to buy anything. You may keep the books and gift and return the shipping statement marked "cancel." If you do not cancel, about a month later we'll send you 6 additional books and bill you just $3.99 each in the U.S., or $4.74 each in Canada, plus 25¢ shipping & handling per book and applicable taxes if any.* That's the complete price and — compared to cover prices of $4.75 each in the U.S. and $5.75 each in Canada — it's quite a bargain! You may cancel at any time, but if you choose to continue, every month we'll send you 6 more books, which you may either purchase at the discount price or return to us and cancel your subscription.

*Terms and prices subject to change without notice. Sales tax applicable in N.Y. Canadian residents will be charged applicable provincial taxes and GST.

If offer card is missing write to: Silhouette Reader Service, 3010 Walden Ave., P.O. Box 1867, Buffalo NY 14240-1867

NO POSTAGE
NECESSARY
IF MAILED
IN THE
UNITED STATES

BUSINESS REPLY MAIL

FIRST-CLASS MAIL   PERMIT NO. 717-003   BUFFALO, NY

POSTAGE WILL BE PAID BY ADDRESSEE

SILHOUETTE READER SERVICE
3010 WALDEN AVE
PO BOX 1867
BUFFALO NY 14240-9952

OFFICIAL OPINION POLL

ANSWER 3 QUESTIONS AND WE'LL SEND YOU
2 FREE BOOKS AND A FREE GIFT!

0074823 |||||||||||| ||||||| ||||||| FREE GIFT CLAIM # **3953**

YOUR OPINION COUNTS!

Please check TRUE or FALSE below to express your opinion about the following statements:

Q1 Do you believe in "true love"?

"TRUE LOVE HAPPENS ONLY ONCE IN A LIFETIME."
○ TRUE
○ FALSE

Q2 Do you think marriage has any value in today's world?

"YOU CAN BE TOTALLY COMMITTED TO SOMEONE WITHOUT BEING MARRIED."
○ TRUE
○ FALSE

Q3 What kind of books do you enjoy?

"A GREAT NOVEL MUST HAVE A HAPPY ENDING."
○ TRUE
○ FALSE

YES, I have scratched the area below.

Please send me the 2 **FREE BOOKS** and **FREE GIFT** for which I qualify. I understand I am under no obligation to purchase any books, as explained on the back of this card.

DETACH AND MAIL CARD TODAY!

335 SDL DZ32   235 SDL DZ4H

(S-SE-03/04)

FIRST NAME   LAST NAME

ADDRESS

APT.#   CITY

STATE/PROV.   ZIP/POSTAL CODE

www.eHarlequin.com

and they would be dumbstruck, incapable of such a simple action.

Now Penelope found herself reaching for her grandmother's too-thin shoulders, lightly touching them.

The older woman turned her tear-filled eyes toward her granddaughter. "Sometimes I just miss her so much," she said.

The comment knocked the breath from Penelope's lungs. Neither of them ever outwardly talked about Mavis's daughter, Penelope's mother. Heather Moon had always been a ghost of sorts that seemed to hang in the house, between them, forever present.

Mavis leaned back against Penelope, surprising her further. She engulfed the older woman in her arms and gently rocked her. "Shh," she said softly, smoothing her grandmother's hair back from her face in a way she distantly remembered her own mother doing for her. "I miss her, too."

"You know, I ask myself over and over again if I could have done something differently. Said something. Asked for help. Maybe then... Perhaps if..." Her voice broke on a sob.

Penelope tightened her embrace. "It's going to be all right."

"It's never going to be all right, Popi. Don't you see that? Don't you understand? Nothing is ever going to be all right again."

Her grandmother's words frightened her. Partly because Mavis had never voiced such a thought before. But mostly because Penelope was afraid she was right.

Chapter Ten

Penelope was jarred awake by a loud banging in the middle of the night. It had taken her a long time to find sleep, and then her dreams had been filled with images of Aidan drifting far away from her, nothing she did bringing him closer.

She snapped upright in her twin bed.

Gram.

It had to be.

She couldn't be sure how long they'd sat in the middle of the living room floor rocking each other, but by the time Penelope had finally let go and stood, her legs had been stiff and she'd had to help her grandmother up. She'd seen Mavis off to bed, tucking her in in much the same way Mavis used to tuck her in. The move had seemed so strange, yet so very right.

Another round of banging. And this time a voice drifted through her closed door along with it. "Miss Moon? Miss Moon, are you here?"

Penelope threw the top sheet from her legs, grabbed her robe and ran into the living room to face the figure standing in the open doorway.

"Mrs. O'Malley? Is that you?" Penelope whispered, holding her robe tightly around her.

Her heart beat triple time as her mind raced through the multiple reasons Edith O'Malley might be paying her a visit in the middle of the night. But only one emerged clear.

Aidan.

Penelope was distantly aware of Mavis stumbling into the living room behind her.

"What is it?" Penelope asked the obviously overwrought woman.

Mavis lit a couple of candles and came to stand next to Penelope.

"It's Aidan," Mrs. O'Malley said, her face looking older than Penelope had ever seen it look. "I'm sorry to come out here so late—it's just that I don't know if Aidan has family, and even if I did, I wouldn't know how to contact them, and seeing as the two of you have been spending so much time together lately…"

Penelope realized the older woman was also in

her nightgown and a robe and that her hair was up in tiny curlers. On the road behind her sat a beige sedan, the engine still running, the headlights slicing through the darkness like search beams.

Penelope reached out and touched the woman's arm. "What *about* Aidan, Mrs. O'Malley? What's happened?"

Edith shook her head a couple of times, as if trying to remember where she was. "He's been arrested."

Ten minutes later Penelope sat in the sedan beside Edith, after throwing on a cotton dress and a pair of sandals. In her lap she clutched her purse containing her savings passbook. Behind her, Mavis was buttoning up a blouse, having insisted on coming along.

"I didn't know what was happening," Edith said, her eyes overly bright as she focused intently on the road into town. "I still don't know what happened. I heard this ominous knocking on the front door, you know? It reminded me of when Sheriff Bullworth—he was sheriff ten years ago—came by to tell me my Harry had had a heart attack while driving back from Toledo and had died."

She gave a visible shudder as Penelope tried to make sense out of what she was saying.

Mavis poked her head between the two seats. "Aidan Kendall, Edith—what happened to him?"

"Oh. Oh! Yes—"

She swerved slightly, and Penelope was glad

that there was no one else on the road at this hour, which according to the green digital dash clock was 3:06 a.m.

"Anyway, it was the sheriff again. Only, this time Sheriff Parker. And he said he wanted to speak to Mr. Kendall. I asked him if it couldn't keep until morning, you know, because this is no time for someone to want a casual conversation. He told me it couldn't wait. When I turned to go get Aidan, he was already dressed and standing on the stairway."

She stopped speaking. Penelope thought it might be because she needed to take a breath. Her blood surged through her veins as she waited.

Edith looked at her. "That's when Sheriff Parker arrested him."

"Just like that?" Mavis asked, incredulous.

"Just like that. He read something from this little card, the Miranda rights I think they're called, you know, that stuff you used to see on *Matlock* about the right to stay silent."

Now Edith went silent.

Penelope had always loved the familiarity of Old Orchard. But as she looked out at the dark, deserted streets now, she felt a foreboding.

She quietly cleared her throat. "Do you know what the charges were, Mrs. O'Malley?"

She shook her head. "No. No, I don't. I didn't even think to ask. Because, because..." She looked directly into Penelope eyes. "Because all I could think about was why Aidan didn't seem surprised. It was almost as if he had expected the sheriff, you know, given the way he was already dressed and everything. And he calmly turned around and offered his hands to be cuffed." She gave a visible shiver. "Then he said something like, 'it's about time,' and then they were gone."

"'It's about time'?" Mavis repeated, clearly as surprised as Penelope. "What kind of thing is that to say?"

Penelope shushed her, wishing she could have convinced her grandmother to stay home. It was taking every ounce of self-discipline she had not to shake.

"He's all right, Mrs. O'Malley?"

"All right? He's been arrested."

"I mean, did he seem like himself?"

Edith shook her head. "He didn't even look like the same man who's lived under my roof for the past year. The man who ate dinner with me almost every night. He looked like someone else entirely."

The car slowed. Penelope peeled her gaze from the older woman's pale face and stared at the sheriff's office. The front window was brightly lit, as it always was, and inside she could make out at least a dozen Old Orchard residents she was surprised to see up this late. She reached for the door handle, clutched her purse, then was out of the car as Edith parked.

Inside the sheriff's office, she sought Cole Parker, who grimaced when he spotted her.

"Penelope. What are you doing here?" asked the sheriff.

Her grandmother and Mrs. O'Malley entered after her.

"I understand you have Aidan in custody," Penelope said.

The sheriff's intelligent eyes took in the three women, and he straightened his shoulders. "That's correct."

"May I ask what the charges are?"

"You may, but that doesn't mean I have to answer."

Mavis pushed by Penelope. "What, are they a state secret or something?"

Penelope opened her purse and fished around for her checkbook. "Tell me how much the fine is."

"Fine?" Sheriff Parker asked.

Penelope found a pen, uncapped it and began filling in a check that didn't include the amount. "For whatever he's done."

Amos McCreary snorted. "He's robbed the General Store, missy. I don't think any check can cover that."

Penelope's hand froze, and the shaking she'd been so good at controlling since she'd first spotted Mrs. O'Malley on her front porch began in earnest. "What?" she whispered.

Sheriff Parker frowned at the other man. "I'm afraid Amos is right, Penelope. Aidan Kendall has been arrested on suspicion of armed robbery. Two counts."

"Two?"

He nodded, then glanced away from her as if unable to continue while looking at her. "That's right. The General Store and Smythe's filling station."

It took her three attempts to shove her checkbook back into her bag, her fingers were trembling so badly. "But…"

The sheriff stepped toward her as if to steer her away from the small crowd. "I know this must come as a shock, Penelope. I swear, I couldn't believe my eyes when I saw the security camera tape." He stopped walking. "It's him. He did it."

"When?" she asked.

He blinked at her. "I don't see—"

"When?" she demanded again. "Did it happen tonight? At what time?"

He scanned her face and sighed. "Tonight. Or rather, last night, now that it's three a.m. That's all I'm going to say."

"Was the store still open? It was, wasn't it? Which makes it before nine p.m." She swallowed hard and lifted her chin. "If that's the case, Sheriff, then you have the wrong man. Because Aidan was with me."

* * *

Aidan's instincts had been right all along. His past had caught up with him. Right here in Old Orchard.

Aidan sat with his forearms resting on his thighs, his head in his hands, trying to make sense out of everything that had led him to where he was right now. Accused of two counts of armed robbery. One at the gas station. The other at the General Store. Perpetrated by a man who looked remarkably like him.

Davin.

His twin brother. A man who resembled him in so many ways. A man who was like him not at all.

A man who wanted to make Aidan suffer.

Correction, make *Allen Dekker* suffer.

A door opened and keys jangled. Aidan absently noticed the sounds without acknowledging them. He'd crawled deep inside himself, trying to figure out what he had done to make his brother hate him so—

"I'm letting you out on your own recognizance."

Aidan lifted his head and stared at Sheriff Cole Parker. "What?"

"You heard me." Cole unlocked the cell door, not looking too pleased with his decision.

Aidan rose unsteadily to his feet. "Why?"

Cole caught and held his gaze. "Penelope Moon insists you were with her at the time of the crime."

Penelope…

Aidan moved purposely forward and grabbed the cell door.

Cole's eyes narrowed. "I figure she's not telling the truth, but she's not budging an inch."

Aidan raked his hand through his hair, wondering what could have compelled Penelope to step forward on his behalf. He looked back at the cell and considered the past two hours he'd spent there. The lifetime he would spend in a similar cell if Davin had his way.

"So are you coming, or not?" Cole asked.

A part of Aidan wanted to tell him to close the door. He didn't want to cause Penelope any problems.

Another part told him he would seal his own fate if he didn't accept this opportunity.

He walked out, his mind crowded with possibilities and ideas…and fear for the woman who had just pointed out her existence to the man who could hurt them all.

Penelope stumbled to her feet from where she'd been sitting next to her grandmother on the front bench, trying to prevent the woman from saying anything that would find her behind bars alongside Aidan. Given her past history with the sheriff's office, Mavis wasn't shy about sharing her feelings about them. Actually, considering Gram's fountain activities, Penelope was beginning to suspect that her grandmother wasn't shy about much of anything anymore.

But after tonight's crying jag, she also knew Mavis was as soft as a Moon Pie inside and that her soul had been bruised irreparably when her daughter took her own life.

"Shh," Penelope said, sensing something was happening. Everyone in the office turned as Cole came from the back. She curled her fingers into her palms as Aidan followed after him.

The room was so quiet, she could hear her heart beat. Especially when Aidan gave her little more than a brief, hard glance and passed her on his way down the street.

Penelope's throat tightened to the point of pain. She seemed to be frozen to the spot, incapable of hearing anything beyond the crash of blood past her ears. Somehow she managed to force her legs to move and she stumbled out of the office after him, blind to everything else around her.

"Aidan?" she said quietly.

He strode purposefully down the dark street away from her.

"Aidan!" she called.

He turned to face her, and they both stood as still as the lampposts that illuminated the night.

"Why did you lie, Penelope?"

She blinked at him, confused, then glanced toward the glass front of the sheriff's office. Mavis and Mrs. O'Malley were watching through the window, along with the sheriff and the others gathered. She managed to move the short distance that would put her out of their line of sight.

"I don't understand…" she whispered.

Why would her convincing the sheriff to let him go until arraignment the following morning upset him?

A brief shadow of sadness moved over his features. But it was gone too quickly for her to respond. She could only think of her first impression of him—that he looked sadder than any man she'd ever seen.

"You risked yourself for me," he said evenly. "I don't ever want you to do that again."

Her knees felt strangely elastic. "I'd do anything to help you."

"And if I had committed those crimes?"

"You couldn't have," she said.

"Who says?" he asked, his dark brows raised ominously. "You? Do you think you really know me well enough to say that I'm incapable of such an act?"

Suddenly he had moved and was standing directly before her, his presence both menacing and reassuring. She swallowed hard.

"Yes," she breathed.

He grasped her arm roughly. "You think so, do you? You think you know me, Penelope?" He leaned in close so that his hot breath swept over her cheek. She shivered in excitement and a hint of fear.

"I know your heart," she said firmly.

His gaze flicked over her face and that sadness again entered his eyes. His fingers released her, but she still felt his touch.

She knew this man's soul as well as she knew her own. Inside and out. And the man she knew could never, would never, have committed the crimes he was accused of.

"What you know can get you hurt," Aidan murmured.

She stared at him.

"You didn't know that, did you?"

She slowly shook her head. "You'd never let me be hurt."

"And if I couldn't prevent it?"

Her mind went blank but for one thought. "Well, then, that's my decision to make, Aidan. Not yours. Not the sheriff's. Not anybody's but my own."

He tore his gaze from hers and appeared ready to step away. She quickly reached out and touched him. "Please. I don't know if I can help. But I want to try."

The sadness in his eyes disappeared, replaced by a brutal void that made her shudder.

"Nobody can help me, Penelope. Not even you."

* * *

A lesser woman would have been gone with his first comment. But not Penelope. Never Penelope. Despite her lack of self-confidence, when it came to others she was there, no questions asked.

Half an hour later Aidan considered Penelope where she stood in Edith O'Malley's foyer along with Edith and Mavis. He paused where he had just descended the stairs, clutching his suitcase tightly and thinking that a lesser woman never would have lied on his behalf.

He'd returned to the bed-and-breakfast with one intention and one intention only. To leave so he wouldn't involve Edith in what was about to happen.

"You're going?" Penelope said hoarsely.

"I'm checking into the motel on the opposite side of town."

He waited to see her relief. When he didn't, he realized that she hadn't expected him to leave. And that having her belief verified merely strengthened her resolve to help him.

"But why should you leave here? Leave this house?" Edith asked, shaking her head and making her curlers rattle. "I don't understand any of this."

Mavis snorted. "None of us do. And he's—" she pointed a craggy finger at him "—too stubborn to fill us in on any of it."

"Wait a minute," Mrs. O'Malley said. "I'll be right back."

Penelope stepped away from her grandmother and met him at the foot of the stairs. "Aidan?"

God, she was beautiful. Not just aesthetically. Oh, no. While Penelope Moon had model-caliber good looks, she didn't try to cash in on them. But that's not what her made beautiful. She was a woman who stood by her family and friends, no matter what. She was strong in her convictions and not about to let anyone sway her from them. He'd watched her with her grandmother, a woman who could be as insufferable as she was lovable. Without blinking an eye, Penelope let Mavis know she would always be there. Always.

She'd also be there for Aidan.

A dull ache began in the pit of his stomach. He recalled thinking of the many reasons why he shouldn't become involved with Penelope. Why he shouldn't give himself over to his attraction to her, his need. And every one of the reasons came back to haunt him now.

When Penelope Moon loved, she loved all the way. There was no halfway for her. And he knew with all his heart that she loved him.

Just as he knew with all his heart that he loved her.

Which was the reason he had to go.

He wasn't leaving town. No. He'd resolved to stay and see this through to the end, once and for all. But he had to do it alone.

"Here," Mrs. O'Malley said, hurrying up the

hall. She held out a large brown paper bag for him. ''Just some leftovers and stuff. You know, so you don't live off that fast food. It's not good for you.''

Aidan accepted the heavy bag. ''Thank you, Mrs. O.'' He kissed her cheek.

He met Penelope's expectant gaze.

''Goodbye,'' he said. And then he did one of the hardest things he'd ever done in his life. He walked away from her.

Chapter Eleven

How was Penelope supposed to carry on with life as usual when everything was so far from normal?

In the back of her shop the following day, she absently wrapped the hand-milled bars of lavender soap she'd made two weeks ago in purple tissue paper, then tied them off with purple ribbon. It was Monday and she'd been open for an hour, but she had yet to receive a single customer. No doubt everyone was as preoccupied with the news of Aidan's arrest as she was.

Of course, she was also the only one who knew there was no way he could have done what he was accused of. She didn't need to know his exact whereabouts at the time of the crime to know that.

Spot jumped up onto the counter, sniffed the covered soap, then twitched her tail at Penelope. Penelope reached out and patted the overfed, black-and-white cat, then put her back down on the floor. Maximus lifted his mammoth head to take in the move, and then laid it back down again. Penelope considered him. If she didn't know better, she would think that the dog had empathetically tuned in to her somber mood and was emulating it.

"What's the matter, boy?" she asked, crouching down to scratch the back of his furry ears. "Not feeling up to par this morning?"

She sighed, thinking she could relate.

The problem was that she didn't think she'd feel up to par ever again.

It was more than just Aidan's shocking predicament. It was his one-hundred-and-eighty-degree turnaround in their relationship. She stood up, absently rubbing the side of her neck. Wasn't it just two nights ago that she'd bared her body and her soul to him and that he'd stroked both with his gentle passion?

Now...

Now he looked at her as if she were a stranger. No...she was more than familiar with that expression, having grown up in Old Orchard as the odd woman out. Rather, he looked at her as if he regretted ever laying eyes on her.

A shiver ran over her skin, then seemed to wiggle under it, making her feel like ten kinds of fool.

And twenty kinds of woman in love, unwilling to accept the object of her affection's blatant rejection.

The bells on the store door rang. Penelope lethargically stacked the wrapped soaps, wiped her hands on a towel, then went out to greet her first customer of the day.

She froze when she saw that it was Elva Mollenkopf, pretending to look at a display of dried herbs, then moving on to the shelves of books on metaphysics, astrology and yoga.

Penelope forced her bravest face. "Good morning, Elva," she said quietly, taking her place behind the cash register and popping open the drawer. "I'm surprised to see you here. Have you run out of face cream already?"

Elva openly glared at her. "No. What I bought should see me through three months." She stepped to the counter. "I came by to ask whether or not you were involved in Mr. Kendall's illegal goings-on."

Penelope felt like she'd been slapped. "Pardon me?"

Elva seemed to take great pleasure in her uneasiness. "I told you there was something 'off' about that man. Sneaking into town the way he did. No one knowing where he comes from.''

"The east.''

Elva's eyes narrowed to slits. "I thought he was from Oregon.''

Penelope's face burned at how easily she'd shared information that only she had known, with a woman who would like nothing better than to hurt Aidan.

"Elva, do you have a family history of depression?''

The woman looked genuinely shocked. "What kind of question is that?''

"A valid one, I think, given your consistent sour behavior.''

"Sour?'' she sputtered.

Penelope nodded. "Yes, I think *sour* about covers it. Tell me, do you sit up all night imagining the ways you can hurt people? Or does it come naturally to you?''

Elva's shock morphed into something far darker. "You're a fine one to talk, missy. You and your weird family doing Lord-knows-what on the outskirts of town. I've heard that the neighbors' small animals go missing at certain times of the year, and later the bones are found.''

Penelope had never heard that one but wasn't surprised. "I wonder who it is that started that rumor.''

She stared at the woman evenly, then turned to

search through her stock of herbal teas. She settled on St. John's Wort. "Are you on any medication, Elva?"

"What?"

"You heard me." She put the box down on the counter and shoved it toward the annoying woman. "If you're not, I'd strongly suggest you drink a cup of this tea every morning."

"I'm not buying—"

"It's a gift. I wouldn't dream of asking you to part with a penny of your precious money. The squeak would probably shatter my delicate eardrums."

Elva's chin went up, she made a sound between a snort and a sigh, and then she stalked toward the door, clutching her purse but without the tea.

The bells rang again as she left. Then silence settled over the shop like a death knell.

Penelope took a deep breath and briefly closed her eyes. She'd never spoken remotely like that to anyone in her entire life. And she wasn't too sure how she felt about having done so now. She eyed the packaged tea, wondering if she should mail it to the nasty old woman. She stacked it back on top of the others, then stared at the door. Pulling Max's leash from the hook on the wall, she went in the back and attached it to his chain collar.

"Come on, boy. We have some unfinished business to tend to."

She turned the Closed sign around on the front

door and let Spot precede them out. Then she locked the door behind herself, closing the shop for the day for the first time in five years.

Aidan hadn't slept for the past thirty hours and the effects were beginning to show. His eyes felt as dry as the salt mines in nearby Perrysburg. His movements were slow and small as if anything more demanding would completely sap him of whatever energy he had left. He leaned back in the uncomfortable motel room chair, trying to read the computer screen without the words running together. Nothing. Nothing at all on his brother Davin and his possible whereabouts.

Of course, Davin was just as good at using computers as he was, so he wasn't surprised that his brother wouldn't leave an electronic trail.

Which made him wonder if *he* inadvertently had.

Leaning forward, he minimized the screen search for his brother's name, positioned the cursor over the browser's search box, then typed in his alias: Aidan Kendall.

With a bleep, one result immediately popped up.

He clicked on the link and stared as a picture of him filled the screen. He read the caption underneath: "New Teacher Gains Praise from Students and Parents Alike."

The photo was one shot taken at the end of the school year—a month ago while he was talking to the parents of the Jones boy. He hadn't even been aware that the photo had been taken, much less that it had appeared in the *Old Orchard Chronicle*.

He pressed the print button, then drew in a deep breath. Well, that explained how Davin had found him. High up on the list of search parameters for him was likely "new teacher." And a glimpse of the photo was all it would take to put Aidan Kendall together with Allen Dekker.

He snatched the printed page out of the hopper and stared at the grainy black-and-white photo. It had taken him two trips to move everything from Mrs. O'Malley's bed-and-breakfast to the motel. And he'd been working on the computer ever since.

Ominous that instead of finding anything on his brother, he'd found something on himself.

He squinted hard at the photo. But why wouldn't Davin just alert authorities? Publicly make the link between Aidan and Allen?

He is playing with me. The way a cat toys with a mouse before moving in for the kill.

Aidan put the printout down and pushed himself out of the chair. The information made him uneasier still.

He'd figured out early on that if he was to stand a chance against his brother, he had to try to think like Davin.

He'd also figured out that he was ill-equipped for the job. How did one go about rationalizing what his brother had done? Explain the motivation behind the ruthless efficiency with which he was deconstructing every part of his twin brother's life? They'd shared a womb together, even a single egg. But from then on, they'd taken completely different paths. Aidan couldn't begin to imagine the road his brother traveled, much less crawl into his mind or his black heart.

Aidan stood stock-still, realizing he was no longer alone in the motel room.

He swung around, half hoping it was Davin.

Instead, he found Penelope standing in the doorway. He'd just opened the door to allow in some fresh air.

She looked better than any one woman had a right to.

Penelope glanced from him to the desk and back again. "I guess you do know how to use a computer."

Penelope breathed a little sigh of relief—because for a brief, unguarded moment she'd seen in Aidan's eyes what she'd seen there before last night. Before the world had come crashing down around her ears, refusing to make sense. Before he'd shut her out.

Along with the relief came a vanishing of her resolve.

Her exchange with Elva had left her determined to take forward steps rather than to remain in the dark. But now that she stood in front of Aidan, saw how tired he was, saw how glad he was that she was there, no matter how hard he tried to hide it, she forgot about everything but her growing need for him on every level.

"What are you doing here?" he asked.

She hesitantly held up a bag. "I asked Trudy at the diner to make an exception to the no-breakfast-after-ten-thirty rule and make you something." He didn't move to take it, so she put it down on the desk next to one of two computers. "You look awful," she said.

"I've felt better."

Outside the door behind her, Max barked at something. She tugged on his leash and fastened the end to the open door handle. He whined at her, then settled down to watch the goings-on outside.

That done, she was forced to confront her fears and Aidan, the two interwoven. "Tell me what's going on, Aidan."

There was a brief hardness to his features, but he didn't appear in any condition to back it up. He sank to the edge of the bed, looking irresistibly handsome and undeniably tired.

"I can't."

"You can't, or won't?" she asked, turning his words back on him.

"Both," he said after a long silence.

She slowly crossed the room and sat down next to him; the casual intimacy made her heart kick up a notch, even though the way things stood between them, they could have been continents apart.

He restlessly ran his hand through his hair several times, tousling the dark strands, making her itch to follow his lead, to feel the rough texture of his hair against her sensitive palms.

"You wouldn't understand," he said.

Penelope kept her gaze level, afraid that at any moment he would shut her back out and she would find herself on the other side of the closed door with no hope of gaining reentry.

"Try me," she whispered.

He turned his head to look at her. The utter sorrow in his eyes nearly took her breath away.

Sensing that he was about to say something she didn't want to hear, she reached for the bag of food and systematically began taking items out. "Here. We all think better with something in our stomachs."

She handed the takeout tray of scrambled eggs, bacon and toast to him, then dared to glance back into his face. She was surprised to find him smiling. Not a full-out, thousand-megawatt Aidan grin, but it would do. It would more than do because it gave her hope.

"Are you always this bossy?"

She stared at him. "Actually, it's something new I'm trying. How's it working?"

He accepted the tray. "I'd give you a *B+*."

"No *A*?"

He shook his head. "No *A*. I rarely give out *A*'s. What are you going to strive for if you've already done the best?"

Indeed, Penelope thought, filled with the urge to smooth his hair back from his troubled brow. Instead, she concentrated on taking the top off the orange juice she held.

Max whined from the door, the smell of bacon apparently gaining his interest. Aidan took a bite of a strip, then tossed Max the rest.

Penelope bit down on her tongue hard to keep from saying anything to break the quiet moment. Aidan was eating. That and his smile were a start. And more than enough for now.

She put the orange juice on the desk, then gathered up the newspapers strewn across the floor and put them into a neat pile. She spotted the large paper bag that Mrs. O'Malley had given him the night before, and looked to find everything still inside.

"No refrigerator," Aidan said.

"You haven't eaten anything since early yesterday?" She swallowed hard. No wonder he looked so bad. "This isn't fit for Max now." She put the bag outside the door so she could toss it in the Dumpster on her way out.

Ten minutes later, she watched Aidan get up, food eaten and orange juice drained, seeming surprised that he'd been hungry. He stood smack-dab in front of Penelope where she had just turned from the door.

She felt suddenly, excitedly alert as she faced him. She fought not to avert her gaze, but to hold his in a way she sensed they both needed right that moment.

How different everything looked now. Where just yesterday the future had appeared alive with possibilities, now she didn't dare look beyond this second for fear of what she might uncover. Oh, no, she didn't for a minute believe that Aidan had done what he was accused of. But she did know that what he had shut her out from, what he was hiding from her even now, was dark and frightening and couldn't be turned away from once revealed.

"You're a sight for sore eyes, do you know that, Penelope Moon?" he said softly.

Tears pricked her eyes at his words. Amazing how something so simple could touch her so deeply.

"And you need some sleep," she murmured, feeling her face go hot.

He lifted a hand to tuck her hair behind her ear, appearing content to just stand there and do nothing but that. Her heart expanded so much that she was surprised her rib cage could contain it.

While he'd never said the words, Penelope sensed Aidan Kendall loved her. Felt it in his touch. Saw it in his eyes. Sensed it with every fiber of her being. And that love fed her love for him until she thought she might spontaneously combust with the power of it.

She leaned forward, pressing her lips first to one side of his mouth, then the other, her actions seeming as natural as the sunrise. She leaned her forehead against his and closed her eyes, inhaling everything that was him.

"Get some rest, Aidan. Whatever you're facing, you won't be able to do it in the state you are now."

"Sleep with me," he said.

Her eyes fluttered open and she pulled back and smiled. "That won't help you, either."

He chuckled softly, his fingers still in her hair. "I know. But damn if I don't want to do it anyway."

"Maybe I could stay for a while—" She cleared her throat. "You know, until you fall asleep."

His smile warmed her to the core. "I'd like that."

He reached to pull his shirt off. She'd felt every inch of him in the dark, but hadn't really seen him. Now she drank in her fill, appreciating every curve of muscle and smooth flesh. His nipples were flat and tan, the hair spattering his chest dark and crisp. He slipped out of his shoes and reached down to take off his socks. He seemed to have trouble keeping his balance.

"Here, let me." Penelope indicated for him to sit back down on the bed. When he had, she knelt

down in front of him, slowly pushing up his pants
legs and gently removing his dark socks. She concentrated on her task, not wanting to jerk or pull
or otherwise jar him further awake. She looked up
to find she was too late. Aidan had lain back
against the mattress and appeared to be sound
asleep.

Gently, she maneuvered him so that his body
was crosswise on the bedspread. She took the extra
pillow and blanket from the closet and put the pillow under his head and the blanket over him, then
moved to check the air conditioner. It didn't work
on low or high, but medium seemed okay. She
stared at the glowing computer screens, finding a
printout of a picture of him that she remembered
from the *Chronicle*. She ran her thumbnail down
the story, recalling it. Remembering how she'd
thought he looked so handsome. She moved her
hand, disturbing a piece of paper near the edge of
the desk. She tried to figure out how to turn off
the computers but gave up.

A sudden *beep* startled her. She leaned back and
saw the words ''search complete'' blink across the
screen, then a sentence appeared: ''Fifteenth An-
niversary of House Fire Cause of Push for Tougher
Building Codes.''

Penelope's breath caught in her throat. What
was Aidan involved in? She glanced over her
shoulder to find him softly snoring, his head turned
away from her. Concentrating her attention back

on the computer, she tried to find a way to access the document. The first button she pushed gave her a list of options. It said to press shift *O*. She did.

And she read in one minute what Aidan hadn't revealed in the past year of knowing her....

Chapter Twelve

At dusk Aidan climbed from the old Chevy he'd
kept parked in Mrs. O'Malley's garage and took in
his surroundings at a gas station near Toledo Metro
Airport, about an hour northeast of Old Orchard.
He felt in charge of his mental faculties again,
thanks to Penelope and the food she'd plied him
with and the sleep she'd made him get. He'd awakened an hour and a half ago with a clear mind and
rested body, to find a home-cooked meal waiting
in a bag on his desk…right next to the computer
showing some vital information he'd been searching for.

Somehow he knew Penelope had viewed it.

He'd performed a simple check of the queue to verify that. But had she understood what it meant? Probably not. For her sake, he hoped she didn't. But to be on the safe side, he'd decided to leave the motel early the next morning and check in someplace else, a little farther away from Old Orchard. Somewhere Penelope wouldn't know where to look. The situation was heating up, and he wanted her nowhere near the danger zone. He'd already lost so much already. He couldn't bear it if he lost her, too.

He crossed to the public pay phone and dialed a number he hadn't called for over a year—since before he'd settled in Old Orchard. Settled coming a little too close to reality for his liking.

He kept his head effectively turned away from any security cameras that the filling station might have aimed in his direction and waited as the phone at the other end rang. Once, twice...

"Hello?"

It had been a long time since Aidan had heard a voice connected to his past. His friend Brody Tanner had been his roommate throughout much of college, his best man at his wedding.

He'd also been the man to step up to the plate when the world had taken away Aidan's family and fingered him as the one responsible.

"The end is in sight," Aidan said simply.

Penelope leaned against the wall outside the closed door to Aidan's motel room. Through a slit in the curtains, she'd verified that his computers still glowed and his clothes were still there, so she knew he would be coming back. The question was, when? And what state would she be in, considering the information burning a hole in her purse?

And considering how much everything had changed with one little innocent bleep of a computer.

A shadow moved on the steps twenty feet to her right. She jumped, then squinted into the post-dusk darkness. It took her a moment to realize that the figure was an animal, not a human, and that the animal in question was Spot.

Max lumbered up to a sitting position, his tail thumping against the wood planks.

"What do you know. You guys are friends now, are you?"

She watched the fearless, curious cat weave around her ankles, then push her head against the fur of Max's chest where he was tethered to the iron railing.

Penelope shook her head and stared out at the still parking lot and the two-lane route beyond. She made out a set of headlights in the distance even as her heart contracted. What she'd unearthed…what she'd discovered…had shocked and confused her. But above and beyond everything else it made her love all the more the man who had so skillfully toppled all of her emotional barriers.

She heard a car door close. She blinked and looked down to find Aidan staring up at her. His face once again wore a worried expression. His posture stiff and unapproachable. Penelope briefly closed her eyes. He was easier to deal with when he was tired and hungry.

"What are you doing here, Penelope?" he asked her, his voice a hard monotone as he came to stand before her.

She suppressed a shiver but didn't respond.

He turned from her, sighed, then opened the door, motioning for her to precede him in, as he gave the parking lot and neighboring doors a hard visual inspection.

When the door closed quietly behind her, the darkness of the room beyond was broken only by the unnatural glow of the computer screens.

Aidan turned to face her without switching on the lights, as if waiting for a response to his question.

Penelope thought her palms might never be dry again. "We need to talk, Aidan—"

He didn't acknowledge that he'd heard her.

"—or should I say *Allen?*"

Damn. She knows.

Aidan glanced at the computer screen and the

article that was still open there. He didn't have to ask how she knew.

She looked so far outside her element that Aidan nearly groaned and gathered her up into his arms to chase away the uncertainty painted across her face. But he couldn't. Not now. Especially since he knew just how much danger they were both in.

She reached for the large purse strap over her shoulder, rustled around inside the depths of the bag and produced a series of papers creased from where she must have stuffed them inside without folding them.

"I went to the library. I, um, didn't know how to use the computer, but Twila helped me out and…" Her voice drifted off.

Aidan accepted the printouts. The first page was a hard copy of the article on the screen. The second was a piece that covered his parents' death in that same house fire fifteen years ago. The third item was…

He cleared his throat of the emotion that nearly choked him.

The third was a picture of him and Davin at thirteen, the year before their parents died. The same picture he had in the frame at the bottom of his suitcase.

"You were young, but that's you, isn't it? That's you in the picture with your twin brother?"

He tossed the printouts, including the picture, to the bed. "Yes," he said, the word seeming to rob him of so much energy, yet making him feel freer than he had in a long time.

How long had it been since he'd been able to share something truthful, something real about himself, his life, his past with anyone else? It seemed like forever. And the ability to do so now was like a salve to his bruised and battered soul.

"He's the one responsible for the robberies. The reason your likeness is on the security video from the General Store."

He stared at her. The questions weren't questions but statements. As if she already believed what he hadn't offered.

He noticed the protective way she stood, with her arms crossed over her torso as if trying to ward off the cold, the dip of her chin against her chest. But it was her eyes, unwavering in her belief, that seemed to unlock a steel door to his heart and allow the love he'd kept hidden inside to come gushing out.

"Yes," he said again.

His palms longed to touch her skin. His nose breathed deeply as if in a quest for a mere whiff of her hair. His body ached for her in a way that would have been frightening in its intensity if he hadn't already identified his feelings for the woman standing in front of him.

He loved Penelope Moon. With ever molecule of air that he breathed in. Every drop of blood that pumped through his heart.

"Tell me," she whispered.

Tell her what? That he loved her?

He shoved his hands deep into his pockets, knowing that's not what she was asking. But there was no doubting that she probably needed to hear it just the same.

But he couldn't tell her. Not now. Maybe not ever.

He could, however, share what she was asking for, seeing as she'd already pieced much of it together by herself.

"Yes, Allen is my real name. Allen Dekker. And Davin is my twin brother. He…" He fell silent. "He and I had always been close. Or at least I thought so. Then…"

She waited patiently, giving him the space he needed to work through his jumbled thoughts, emotions.

He walked across the room to stand in front of the windows. For several moments he said nothing. Then he felt Penelope's hand on his shoulder.

"Tell me, Aidan. Tell me what happened."

He wanted to. He did. Only, he didn't know where to start.

He cleared his throat, and when he spoke his voice was barely above a whisper. "When our parents were killed in a house fire, we both went to live with my father's brother in a small town outside of Providence." He remembered the move as if it were yesterday. He and Davin had still been wearing the plain black suits a next-door neighbor had bought for them. Their suitcases had been stowed in the bed of the old truck behind them, stuffed full of everything they could fit in. "It was hard in the beginning. But as time went on and we settled in, I thought…I thought everything was all right. That being with family was better than being split up, no matter how different everything was." His words trailed off as he tried to piece everything together for her in a way that wasn't too confusing.

"Much later I discovered that while I was leading a relatively normal life, Davin was being subjected to mental and physical abuse I couldn't begin to fathom. Not then, not now."

He shook his head, still wondering how he couldn't have known. How he could have bought Davin's excuses about the bruises on his face, the hard silences at the dinner table.

"He'd always been the more rebellious of the two of us. And I knew my uncle was disciplining him. But I didn't have any idea how brutal that discipline was."

Penelope nodded her understanding.

"Then we went off to college together, and Davin's behavior became more bizarre. He'd turn in papers pretending he was me and I'd get a failing grade. I'd start dating a girl and he'd sleep with her, pretending to be me." He wouldn't share that he suspected Davin had committed at least one date rape under his name. Thankfully, by then the dean had more than an inkling of what was going on and disciplined them both. Because the girl in question refused to bring them up on official charges, a temporary suspension was the most that the public university could do. The girl left campus. The twins stayed on, this time with Allen determined to keep a closer eye on his brother.

And what he had seen turned his stomach.

Davin had always been a rambunctious child, and friendly around Aidan, but Aidan had quickly discovered a dark, vicious side to his twin that seemed to stem directly from their being so closely tied together. Shortly thereafter he transferred to another college, hoping the physical distance would force Davin to start living his own life rather than being obsessed with Aidan's.

He didn't find out that Davin had dropped out of college altogether and followed him, shadowing every step of his life, until it was much too late.

He shared most of his thoughts with Penelope, trying to be fair, carefully choosing what to tell her and what to keep to himself. Still, even now, he felt somehow oddly responsible for his brother's behavior—even though he didn't think he could hate another human being more for what he had done.

Aidan paced across the room, then back again, this time reaching out to close the curtains. "I met my wife during my senior year at Columbia." He had his back to Penelope, but he could feel her gaze as strongly as a touch. "I remember thinking my life was perfect. From my second year on, I'd worked as a substitute teacher at a local junior high, then a teacher's assistant at the university, and there I was going to graduate with an engineering degree and had already secured an internship with a major defense contractor in Virginia." He closed his eyes, remembering the carefree time. Remembering the exact shade of blonde that Kathleen's hair was, the flash of her smile, the sound of her laughter. "Kathleen was a month away from becoming a CPA. And within three months of our first meeting we got married before the justice of the peace."

The silence in the room seemed to press in on him from all sides.

"So we moved to Virginia and for the next four years made a home, built a nest egg and tried like hell to conceive a baby."

His throat threatened to choke off his words, the gravity of what he was about to say twisting his gut, making him want to hide, stop there and not go on, not blacken Penelope's heart with the tragedy that had stolen his soul.

But even more powerful than that was his need to share the reality that had been his life for what seemed like forever.

He closed his eyes, his voice growing lower still. "After the third year we decided to be tested. I'd just gone in when I came home to find Kathleen crying. She was pregnant." His voice grew so low that he wondered if she could hear him. "I thought her tears were ones of joy. But the next week I got the results of my test and found out I suffered from a blockage making it nearly impossible for me to have fathered any children without a medical procedure. I confronted Kathleen and she broke down and told me Davin had raped her."

Penelope gasped. "Oh, Aidan..."

He heard her move, but he didn't know where until he felt the gentle touch of her hand on his arm.

"I'm so sorry."

He clamped his eyes shut against the memory of the heartbreaking anguish that had been in Kathleen's eyes. Recalled her sadness as her belly grew large with a child conceived in violence. She'd been horrified by the thought of pressing charges against a man they couldn't even prove was in town, much less had raped her. He'd explored the matter on his own—until the D.A. had told him that identical twin DNA was, well, identical and that a rape case would be next to impossible to prosecute. So he'd transferred to another company in Mississippi, moved into a house in a well-guarded community, put in the best security system imaginable, all the while terrified he would lose Kathleen to depression.

"Then Joshua was born and chased all the darkness away with his innocent smile and happy laughter.''

Penelope's heart throbbed heavily for the man with his back to her. She couldn't imagine facing what he had. Couldn't fathom having a brother who would go to such lengths to sabotage her life.

''We were a family again...''

But for how long? Penelope wanted to ask.

She already knew the answer. For much too short a time...

Aidan remained quiet. Penelope didn't indicate her need for him to tell her more. She lightly caressed the rock-hard muscles of his shoulder through his soft T-shirt, trying to ease the tension there. Wanting more, but forcing herself to settle for what he'd given her.

He'd already shared so much. She didn't understand why it was so important to her that he tell her the rest. Or maybe she did. Because the rest was so very intimate. It would come from the depths of his heart. It would take a great deal of strength for him to say the words.

And it would indicate an utter trust in her that would complete the tentative bonds that tied them together.

She didn't realize she'd tightly closed her eyes, praying for him to take that step, until he turned toward her, forcing her hand off his shoulder. He gazed at her in the dim light from the computer, his face drawn in hard, handsome lines. Sadness dwelled there, in his eyes, and seemed to reach out and tangle her in its vine-like tentacles.

He lifted a hand and so tenderly caressed the side of her face that tears flooded her eyes.

"I've been dead for so long now, Penelope, my heart felt like a leaden weight. Until you. Until you touched me with your magic fingers and coaxed it and me back to life."

She dropped her gaze.

"I tried to keep you at arm's length. I tried to block you out. But you wouldn't let me." His fingers slowly moved from her face to her hair. "I'd been living in a monochrome hell for the past year, and you splashed your buckets of vivid color over it until I started to see things clearly again. More than just clearly. I started to see, period." He rested his fingers at the back of her neck, his voice and words caressing her. "I started to see you."

He leaned forward and brushed his warm lips against hers. "Stay with me tonight, Penelope."

Pure, unadulterated need surged through her veins. How she wanted this man. Physically. Emotionally. Soulfully. She wanted him to possess her and in exchange to possess him. She wanted to feel his hard body moving gently over hers, filling her, stroking her. She wanted him to make love to her until nothing made sense, until everything made sense.

"Yes," she breathed more than said, then opened her mouth to allow him in.

Within a heartbeat the tentative meeting of mouths transformed into a hungry assault between two battle-scarred warriors. She, the town outcast who had resigned herself to a life lived on the fringes, not participating, merely an observer. He, a man who had experienced so much sorrow that she couldn't help but feel it whenever she looked at him, whenever he touched her.

He tugged on the cotton of her dress until he could pull it up over her head, mussing her hair so it hung in her face. She reached for his T-shirt and did the same, pressing her hot palms against the planes of his hard abdomen. Aidan restlessly smoothed his fingers over her face, brushing stray strands of hair back so he could kiss her again, even as she stepped out of her panties, and pushed his jeans down over his lean legs.

Then they were standing completely naked in front of each other, baring more than skin as each visually took the other in. Penelope gasped when he lightly touched her right breast, brushing the pad of his thumb over the aching tip. His manhood stood proud and thick and pulsing against his stomach. She reached for it, fascinated by his obvious want of her, desire for her. Moisture beaded the top and she pressed her fingers against it, then rubbed it over the thick knob and down the long, hard length. He made a deep sound in his throat, then caught her hand between them as he grasped her hips and pressed her to him.

Where their last time had been about the first flush of intimacy, this was about fundamental need. A reaching out not just of bodies, but of the very essence that made each of them who they were. Who they were apart, and who they became together.

Aidan edged her toward the bed and leaned down to pull the satiny bedspread from the mattress. It pooled at their feet with the mellowest of whispers. Then he swept Penelope up into his arms. She gasped and grasped his hard shoulders, allowing him to lay her across the bed.

She wasn't a slip of a woman that could easily be picked up. Yet he laid her against the white sheets like that's exactly what she was. And for a moment, a brief, precious moment, that's what she felt like.

His hard body covered hers, his knee gently nudging hers apart, his arms braced on either side of her head as he held her gaze. He brushed her hair from her face, staring at the dark strands as if endlessly fascinated by them. Then he bent and kissed her, coaxing the sparks ricocheting around inside her into a full-out fire.

And beginning the journey to heaven and beyond…

Chapter Thirteen

Two hours later, Penelope seemed helpless to staunch the flow of tears streaming down her cheeks. Aidan gently withdrew from her, knowing the tears were of joy and pleasure even as he kissed them from her skin, tasting the salt on his tongue. He felt connected to Penelope in a way he had never expected to feel connected to another woman. The thought gladdened him, yet was also the cause for great concern.

It was somewhere past midnight now, and the only sounds were of Max's chain collar as he scratched himself on the landing outside the door, and the hum of the computers. He gently wiped the wetness from Penelope's sweet cheeks and bent down to kiss her again, so utterly consumed by his love for her that it was sometimes difficult to breathe.

She opened her eyes and lifted a hand to her face, appearing surprised to find tears there.

Aidan reluctantly rolled to lie next to her, both of them staring at the ceiling. He curled his fingers around hers, feeling the rasp of the ever-present leather tie around her wrist and its unidentified charm.

"I want you to leave town for the time being, Penelope." His voice broke the silence. "Leave Old Orchard. Find someplace safe."

She attempted to move her hand in automatic response and he tightened his grip.

"Where would I go?"

"I don't know. To family, maybe?"

There was a long silence, then she whispered. "Outside Mavis, I don't have any family."

He turned his head to gaze at her, realizing they shared more than he had thought possible.

With the death of his aunt and uncle a few years ago, essentially he was also alone in the world.

Except for Davin.

Except for Penelope.

"Then, go as far as you can as fast as you can. Rent a motel room. Something, anything away from here."

She didn't say anything.

He realized he was brushing his thumb back and forth along the silky skin of her side. He pulled her hand up and pressed his lips against her knuckles, keeping them there for a long time.

"Promise me," he said.

She didn't say anything.

He moved her hand until it pressed against the side of his face.

"Promise me."

"I can't," she said hoarsely.

They lay like that for a long time. Then he felt her move. She rolled to her side to face him, then tugged her hand away. He squinted at her in the dark, discerning that she was doing something with her bracelet.

"My mother gave this to me many years ago," she said quietly, somberly. She held it up so that the charm dangled in front of him. "Do you know what that is?"

Aidan made out a round blue stone with a black dot in the middle of a white one, the stone edged with silver.

"It's a Greek eye. It's supposed to ward off all evil," she whispered.

Before he knew her intention, she was tying it around his left wrist. "I want you to promise me you won't take it off until this is over."

He studied her in the dim light. The way her silky black hair kept sliding into her face and the way she easily tucked it back again.

"What's going to protect you?" he asked.

She smiled at him, a flash of white in the darkness. "You."

He started to pull away, but she stayed him with an arm around his waist, her leg across his.

"Tell me the rest, Aidan."

They both knew that there was more to the story—only, he wasn't sure he was up to sharing it. Given the raw state of his emotions after making love to Penelope for the past two hours, he was loath to let anything taint the sweet love that seemed to encircle them.

But no matter how hard he wished, he couldn't hold at bay the darkness that lurked outside the room.

"Fourteen months ago my brother discovered that my son was his son. Fourteen months ago he killed Kathleen and framed me for the murder."

His words were sharp and clear and caused Penelope to react and gasp in a way that made even him shudder.

The conflicting emotions that had ceaselessly roiled in his stomach until he'd opened himself up to Penelope bubbled to the surface again. So much hate. So much tragedy.

"DNA tests were run. My attorney, my best friend, called to tell me the police were coming to arrest me. So I got out of the house as soon as I could. I've been on the run ever since."

He realized Penelope held on to his hand as if

her life depended on it. As if, if she let go, he might disappear again.

"I moved from town to town. Never staying in one place for more than a week. Never knowing when Davin or the authorities might catch up with me. Never knowing if there was even a reason for me to be running at all. When I came home and found Kathleen…" He flexed his jaw so tightly his teeth ached. "She was my life. There really was no reason for me to go on."

"But you did," Penelope said softly.

"Yes. I did." He stared at the shifting shadows on the ceiling as a car pulled into the parking lot outside. "Because beneath my self-loathing and grief was a single-minded desire to make Davin pay for what he'd done."

She shivered again and he looked at her.

"No, not in the way you think. I don't want to exact any personal revenge on him. I want to see him in prison for the rest of his life." He fell silent for a long while, then said, "I searched for him at first. But there was no trace. No land deeds. Not even IRS records showing he'd worked anywhere. Nothing. The best I can figure is that he's working under an alias…like me."

"But he found you."

"Yes, he found me. And his robbing the gas station and General Store is probably a pretty good indication of how he's funded himself all this time."

"While you went to work to support yourself."

He nodded. "In the beginning I did dishes, bussed tables, even tended bar. All for cash. Until I came here and filled in the temporary position at St. Joe's. I gave them a false social security number and was called on it two months ago. I told the principal that it had to be some sort of clerical error and that I'd look into straightening the matter out. There was no cause for him not to believe me. I'd already become a part of the community."

The sheets rustled as she curled closer to his side. "Was it the picture of you in the paper that led Davin here?"

Her warmth seemed to seep through his skin and reach for his bones. "That's my guess. He knew I'd done some teaching. And he's as good with a computer as I am. Maybe even better. So as soon as the piece was listed on the Internet along with the picture, he probably had it in his hands."

She gestured toward the computers on the desk. "Is that what you do? Search for information on him?"

He nodded. "Yes. It didn't occur to me until yesterday to do a search on myself."

Her smooth shoulder was within kissing distance. He pressed his lips against her smooth flesh and closed his eyes.

"So you think he's followed you here to what... Finish the job?"

His eyes remained closed as he rubbed his nose

against her silken skin. ''That's my best guess. He robbed the gas station hoping that Old Man Smythe's word would be enough to pull me in. When it wasn't, he hit the General Store, which clearly has a security camera, so the sheriff would have to arrest me then. And when he did...''

She made a soft strangled sound. ''And when he did, sooner or later he'd link you to the previous crime. The murder of your wife.''

Aidan didn't say anything. Didn't have to. There it was. All laid out in eye-popping Technicolor.

He shifted her until she lay on her side away from him, then spooned against her back, squeezing her against him. Such a simple action with such a heart-pounding effect.

The phone on the bedside table rang.

Aidan's throat tightened.

Penelope moved. ''Maybe someone's complaining about Max?'' she asked, but with little conviction.

''Maybe.'' He swung his legs over the side of his bed and reached for his jeans, letting the extension ring four times before snatching it up.

''Hello?''

''Oh, thank God you're there!'' Mrs. O'Malley's voice rushed over the line. ''Do you know where Penelope is? Mavis has been attacked....''

Yet again Penelope rode through the night in the passenger seat of a car staring at the town as if it were no longer familiar to her. Where before it had seemed strange, now it loomed ghostly, too many shadows for someone to hide in—too many shadows, period.

She shivered, and Aidan reached out his hand to take hers. "Are you all right?"

She nodded. "It's not me I'm worried about."

Aidan tightly gripped her hand. "I want you to take your grandmother and leave town. Now. Tonight."

She shuddered again, the night seeming very cold even though the temperatures were in the balmy seventies.

"Promise me, Penelope," he said sternly.

"Okay," she whispered. "I promise."

They drove the rest of the way across town to the bed-and-breakfast in silence, the streets deserted, the lights casting an unnatural glow against the building fronts, changing the color of the red brick to dark brown. Aidan finally pulled to a stop a block away from Mrs. O'Malley's house.

"You're not coming with me?" she asked, panicking.

"No. I can't."

He tried to take his hand from hers but she grasped it more tightly. "Where will you go?"

"Back to the motel. I...I just don't think it's a good idea to involve anyone any further in what's happening. There's no telling what Davin's capable of. The farther away I stay from you all, the safer you'll be."

"You weren't around Mavis and she was hurt."

"That's why I want you both to leave."

"And Mrs. O'Malley?"

He looked as if she'd physically assaulted him. "Try to take her with you."

Oh, God. "Oh, Aidan," she said vehemently, flying across the seat and enveloping him in her arms. "You don't have to do this alone." She kissed his neck. "We can all leave town together."

"And then what? Pray we don't get a speeding ticket?" He shook his head. "No, Penelope. This is where this is going to end."

She urgently searched his eyes. "Then, we'll go to the sheriff. Before he links you with your real identity. Explain everything. He'll believe us. He'll help."

Aidan's gaze was steady on her. "Will he, Penelope?"

She didn't know. Everything was all so confusing. The complicated past swirling to muddy the complicated present.

"No one else has. Why would he?"

She hated that he made sense. Hated that she was torn between needing to see to her grandmother and needing to help him. Hated that when he drove off, she might never see him again.

"Penelope," he said.

A sob welled up from her throat.

"Penelope, look at me," he said more firmly. He caught her face in his strong hands and forced her eyes parallel to his. "I want you to know something—"

She quickly put her hand over his mouth. "No! Don't say anything now. Tell me later." She slowly removed her hand, half afraid he might say it anyway. "Don't you dare act like this is the last time we'll see each other, do you hear me, Aidan Kendall?"

He caught her up in a fierce hug, and her tears fell freely down her face, scalding her cheeks, searing her chest.

He set her away from him. "Go," he said, his gaze turned away from hers.

"Aidan."

He reached across her and opened the door. "I said go, damn it. Before either of us says something we'll regret."

As if in slow motion, she slid over and got out of the car. She opened up the back to take Max and Spot out, and had barely closed the door when the tires of the car screamed against the asphalt in Aidan's hurry to disappear into the night.

She stood there staring after him until he was gone from sight. Then she reached into her purse for a handful of tissues and mopped at the mess of her face.

Max whined and laid his head against her upper thigh. Spot rubbed against her opposite leg.

And Penelope had never felt more alone.

Five minutes later she rounded the corner to Mrs. O'Malley's street and climbed the steps. The door immediately swung inward. "Oh, thank God you're here!" Edith said, rushing out to take her arm. "I didn't know what to do. Mavis just showed up at my door, barely able to keep herself upright, almost incoherent and saying that someone had broken into the house and knocked her lights out."

Penelope tried to take in Edith's words. Edith took her curious gaze as something else entirely.

"Your grandmother's words, not mine."

Penelope didn't understand.

"Never mind. Come in, come in. I put her upstairs in one of the guest rooms. She refused to go to the hospital. Said that a good night's sleep was the best prescription for whatever ailed you. But I was afraid she had a concussion and the sheriff agreed, and…"

Mrs. O'Malley's words ran one into the next, but Penelope's mind arrested when she stepped into the foyer to find Sheriff Cole Parker standing there, his hat in his hands, his expression flat.

"Where's Aidan, Penelope?" he said, cutting Edith off. "Or should I say, Allen Dekker?"

Chapter Fourteen

Penelope helped her grandmother sit forward so she could put another pillow behind her back. Then she handed her a glass of water and a couple of aspirin. *Good for whatever ails you,* Mavis had said.

Uncharacteristically traditional advice from a woman who made a life out of being untraditional. Something wrong? She would pull a plant out of the garden, boil it, then make you drink it—different plants for different symptoms—hard to remember and even harder to duplicate. But Penelope had spent her entire life studying her grandmother's homeopathic remedies, then making them to sell to her customers.

Did Mavis's change of heart mean she should clear the shelves of herbal remedies and stock bottles of aspirin, instead?

Or had the whack her grandmother took to the head knocked a couple of marbles loose?

Penelope carefully sat down on the bed next to Mavis. "Tell me what happened."

Mavis handed her back the glass, and she put it down on the bedside table. The old woman shrugged her skinny shoulders, which looked even thinner under the large nightgown that Mrs. O'Malley had loaned her.

"Do you need anything else?" Edith asked from the open doorway.

Penelope didn't have to look. She knew the sheriff was standing outside in the hall behind Edith. But just as she'd ignored him when she'd come inside the house, she ignored him now.

"No, thank you, Mrs. O'Malley." She looked in her direction. "Could you close the door, please?"

Edith looked uneasily at the sheriff.

"I'll be waiting downstairs, Penelope," he said.

He could do what he wanted. She didn't care. She was emboldened by the truth and the need to protect the two most important people in her life. She didn't have time or energy to consider the sheriff's agenda.

The door clicked closed and she looked at her grandmother again. Mavis appeared well enough, but for the paleness of her skin and a huge bump at the base of her skull.

Her grandmother made a face. "What do you want me to say? That it was a mistake to have taken the doors off?" she asked, as defiant as ever.

"No. I want you to tell me what happened."

She shifted, readjusting the bedding across her waist. "Well, I suppose that's easy enough. I heard a sound. Thought maybe it was just you coming in, so I got up to see where you'd been and *wham.* Somebody knocked my lights out."

What went without saying was that, had there been any lights on, maybe the incident wouldn't have happened.

"Is anything missing?"

"What's there to take? I don't think anyone would be interested in the few pieces of old furniture we have left. Or the pictures of your mother. I checked your door before I left to come here and it was still tightly locked, so they didn't take anything from there."

Fear waded up in Penelope's throat. She didn't like the sound of this. She didn't like it at all.

One of the benefits of living in a town the size of Old Orchard was that violent crime was practically nonexistent. She couldn't remember the last time there had been a murder or a rape. Graffiti on the high school wall? It was probably the Polaski twins. Mowed over rural mailboxes? The Dunwoody boys were up to their old tricks.

Mavis getting blindsided?

Aidan's brother Davin was making his move.

Penelope rubbed at the tension knot building up in her forehead. But what move was Davin making by accosting her grandmother? It didn't make any sense.

"You know something," Mavis said simply.

Penelope looked up to find the old woman staring at her.

"You know who did this, don't you. Who knocked my lights out."

"I think the correct term is 'punched your lights out,' Gram, and since you weren't punched, your lights are fine."

"And you're changing the subject."

"There is no subject." She got up from the bed and paced to the window overlooking the dark and empty street. But was it truly empty? Was Davin out there somewhere even now, watching, waiting?

"It's connected to Aidan, isn't it. Some criminal friends of his have tracked him down."

She looked over her shoulder at her grandmother. "Aidan doesn't have any criminal friends." That much was true. But he did have one darkly criminal identical twin brother who shared the same DNA and was capable of Lord knows what.

She turned back toward Mavis. "How's your cousin in Fort Wayne?" she asked.

"What? What kind of question is that to be asking right now, for cripe's sake?"

Penelope gathered up the nightgown Mavis must have changed out of and left on the floor, and put it on a nearby chair. "I'm just thinking you're long overdue for a visit."

Mavis stared at her. "Oh, no." She pointed a finger at her. "The first action that happens in this town for half a century and you want me to leave town?" She shook her head. "Ain't gonna happen."

"Even if you're the victim of that action?"

Mavis narrowed her eyes. "Am I? The victim of it, I mean?"

Penelope sighed. "In an indirect way, yes."

"So this *is* connected to Aidan."

Penelope wanted to scream. Instead, she walked to the door and quickly opened it, hoping that the sheriff wasn't listening outside. He wasn't. She quietly closed the door again and stood there with her hand pressed against the smooth wood.

Mavis's heavy sigh seemed to suck all the air from the room. "You know, that's the problem with us Moons. No conflict."

Penelope closed her eyes. "What are you talking about now?"

She heard the sheets rustle and imagined her grandmother shrugging again. "Peace. Serenity.

Living one with nature. That's what we call living on the outskirts of town. A part of but not active in the community. Keeping to ourselves. It's all a load of crap. I realize that now.''

Penelope slowly turned to face the old woman, wondering if she'd been hit harder than she'd first thought.

"I'm serious," Mavis said, holding her gaze. "You, me. Your mother before you. My mother and grandmother before me." She gestured with her hand. "We studied the cabala. Mapped out the stars. Charted our astrological courses. Experimented with plants. Did yoga. Chanted. For what? For a peace we never really achieved."

"Gram—"

Mavis held up her hand. "No, no. I think I'm onto something here. My head hurts like the dickens, but I've got to follow this through to its natural conclusion."

She stopped talking, and Penelope did as her grandmother had requested and waited, feeling the woman might actually be hiding a point somewhere in her words.

"Without conflict, there is no true life."

Penelope shivered. She absently rubbed her bare arms to smooth the goose bumps rising there.

"We get up at the same time every morning, go to bed the same way. We eat the same foods, boil the same herbs. Season in, season out, we've become more predictable than those we think we're trying to be better than.'' Mavis wasn't really looking at Penelope anymore, rather she appeared to be searching her mind. "We don't have friends. Neither of the female nor male variety. Oh, no. To do so would disrupt our biorhythms. Shatter the peace…'' Her voice drifted off. "Waiting to die. That's all we're doing. Biding our time until the big pink Cadillac in the sky comes for us.''

Her eyes seemed to focus again. "But we're already dead, aren't we? In a sense, we're the walking dead.''

Penelope looked away, unable to hold her grandmother's gaze.

"I don't know what you're involved in or what Aidan's involved in. But follow your heart, Popi. Don't hide anymore. Go for what you want and hold on to it with both hands.''

Penelope's knees felt suddenly incapable of holding her. She felt Mavis staring at her.

"Tell me. Tell me what's going on. Make me feel alive again. Make me feel that tomorrow the sun won't rise in the same spot. Make me feel we're part of the living.''

Penelope stood quietly for what felt like a long moment, unsure how to respond to her grandmother's request, her heart pounding loudly in her ears.

Then she crossed the room, sat on the opposite side of the bed and proceeded to tell Mavis everything.

* * *

An hour and a half later Penelope tucked the sheet around her grandmother's sleeping form and quietly left the room. She had no idea what time it was but knew it was late. She made her way silently down the stairs, careful not to wake Mrs. O'Malley, only to find the sheriff dozing in a chair near the front door.

She paused. To wake him or not to wake him. That was the question.

She reached out and touched his shoulder.

He jerked awake so suddenly he made her jump.

"You, um, must have fallen asleep," she said quietly.

"What time is it?" He glanced at his watch.

Penelope crossed her arms over her chest, watching him rub the sleep from his eyes and get up to face her.

"Where's Aidan Kendall, Penelope?"

She told him that Aidan was at the motel on the opposite side of town.

He shook his head. "No, he isn't. My men drove over about an hour ago after Mrs. O'Malley finally gave in and told us where he'd been staying—and he was long gone. No trace."

Penelope's heart skipped a beat. "Then, I don't know where he is."

He grimaced at her.

"All right, then."

He was moving to open the door when Penelope

touched his arm. "Wait—" She looked through her purse for the printouts from the motel and held them out to him. "Aidan...Allen didn't do what he's accused of, Sheriff."

"That's for a judge and jury to decide, Penelope. Not you or me."

Penelope held the papers out farther. "Just look over these, will you? And if you have any questions, you know where to find me."

"You're going back to the house?"

She nodded. "Where else would I go?"

She breathed a mental sigh of relief when he took the papers and put them in his front pocket.

"Let me give you a lift."

And the endgame begins...

Aidan tried to stretch the tension from his neck, hating to think of all this as a game. But to catch Davin, he had to think like him, and he suspected this was all a game to his brother. A dark and deadly game—and Davin was now the target.

Dawn had broken and he'd spent the night in the front seat of his car, parked to the side of the road and behind a thicket of trees across the street and slightly up the road from Penelope's house. He'd watched the sheriff drop her off at around two a.m., then had heard banging. He'd gotten out of the car and rounded the house in the dark, watching as Penelope boarded up the back door, then lifted the hammer to do the same to the front.

Only, she'd had second thoughts and instead blocked the opening with a sheet of plywood that left a couple of inches open at the top, then moved furniture behind it.

He hadn't dared fall asleep. The sheriff's office had obviously made the connection between Aidan Kendall and Allen Dekker, evidenced by the squad cars he'd watched swoop down on the motel in his rearview mirror as he drove down the road in the opposite direction. The timing dared him to think that luck was on his side. He squinted up into the lightening sky and wondered if, perhaps, someone was looking out for him.

He clenched his teeth, thinking of the life he once knew, the woman he once loved, the family he once had. All of it lost now.

Penelope had helped heal him with her gentle touch. He knew a part of him would always love his late wife, knew she'd always be with him. But he was coming to learn that that didn't mean he couldn't love again. In fact, it was the memory of that love that compelled him to want to love again.

He smiled faintly. Kathleen would have liked Penelope. She would have been fascinated by her quirkiness and would have talked her into letting her natural beauty shine through instead of hiding it behind muted cotton dresses.

But if Kathleen were alive, he never would have met Penelope.

He ran his hands roughly over his face, pondering the strangeness of life and the way it worked. The future was a road that twisted and turned, forcing a change in scenery and lifestyle and outlook, turning the truth into lies and the lies into truth.

And what was the truth now?

He had to find Davin before his twin found him.

And before the sheriff could put him behind bars where he would never be able to prove his innocence and make the man who had taken so much from him pay for his unforgivable crimes.

He heard a loud noise and snapped upright. Across the street Penelope was moving aside the board she'd placed in front of the door. She stepped out onto the porch—looking more beautiful than the last time he saw her—and squinted up into the sunrise, then reached down to pat Max, who had come out of the house to stand next to her.

Aidan's heart hurt just looking at her.

And his hands itched with the overwhelming desire to touch her.

She disappeared back inside the house, then reappeared moments later with Max's leash—heading off, he suspected, to her shop.

The normal action caught him off guard as he watched her walk down the road against the traffic.

He'd known deep down that she wouldn't leave town, even though he'd made her promise that she would. If they had planned for her to stay, he probably would have counseled her to go about her life much as she did every day. Because if Davin was watching—and Aidan was sure he was—he would be looking for any breaks in routine. Planning for them. Then acting on them.

"Smart move, Penelope," he was surprised to hear himself say aloud.

So long as she stuck to her routine, she would be safe.

Still, that hadn't stopped him from making a quick phone call to the sheriff's office earlier that morning and asking them to keep an eye out for her—even though the squad car driving by every half hour put him at risk.

He turned the key in the ignition and listened as the old Chevy revved to life. Now it was time for him to start some looking of his own....

Chapter Fifteen

The hardest thing Penelope had ever done was to go on pretending her life wasn't turned upside down. She'd gone to the shop a little earlier than normal, had tried like crazy to lose herself in the packaging of soaps, the filling of sachets and the mixing of potpourri, all the while with her eye on the street outside, her ear listening for the telephone's ring and her heart solidly with Aidan, wherever he was.

Late in the afternoon, as she made her way toward St. Joe's for the last Fourth of July planning meeting, she wondered if anything would ever look the same to her again. She couldn't even remember the woman she'd been just a week ago, the one with her eyes firmly on the sidewalk in front of her, not daring to look to the left or the right for fear of what she might find there. Not that there had loomed a real fear then. She knew how stupid she'd been before, now that there was a real fear in the form of Aidan's twin brother Davin. A man who had wreaked havoc on Aidan's life, harmed her grandmother and was capable of doing only Lord knew what now.

She tucked the bag that had held the clothes she'd just dropped off at the dry cleaner's into her purse, then tugged on Max's leash—he was considering lifting his leg, appropriately enough, on the fire hydrant outside the sheriff's office. She looked through the front glass at George Johnson and met Sheriff Parker's gaze. He nodded briefly and she nodded back, mildly surprised that he didn't come out to grill her again over Aidan's whereabouts.

Then again, she'd been there in plain sight all day. Except for a short while after ten when she'd gone to Mrs. O'Malley's house to check on Mavis.

She shook her head. *Mavis.* Would there come a time when the old woman wouldn't surprise and shock her? She'd gone to the bed-and-breakfast expecting...well, she hadn't known what to expect. But not anywhere on the list was finding her with Edith O'Malley, drinking coffee and demolishing cream puffs in the kitchen, laughing about something Penelope wasn't privy to and wasn't sure she wanted to be because it had something to do with the shape of the sweets they were eating and the male anatomy.

She'd like to say that her grandmother looked normal. But *normal* wasn't a word she would place in the same sentence as *Mavis*.

Given what her grandmother had done to the house, she had half expected her to be taking apart Edith's kitchen table, tossing her geraniums in the garbage or pounding holes in her walls. Instead she looked—Penelope reached for the right word—happy.

She slowed her step. Is that what it was? Was her grandmother finding a stretch of happiness in a lonely life that she had questioned only the night before?

If so, what did that mean for Penelope?

She picked up her step again and turned the corner, caught up short when Max stopped in the middle of the sidewalk. She stared at him, puzzled.

"What is it, Maxy boy?" she asked, crouching down to pat the dog.

He growled, his eyes fixed straight ahead.

Icy fear crept down Penelope's back. Never once in the two years since she'd found Maximus abandoned on her front porch had she heard him growl.

She anxiously scanned the street in front of him, wondering if he'd seen a squirrel or a cat other than Spot. She hoped for something, anything other than the possibility that Davin Dekker was lurking in the early evening shadows.

No squirrel, no cat, not even a blowing leaf.

Penelope swallowed hard. Then she stiffened and slowly stood. She didn't see anything out of the ordinary. But that meant absolutely nothing. While Max hadn't proven himself an exemplary watchdog, she trusted his instincts. If he thought there was a threat nearby, then there was. But she didn't think that threat would materialize in the form of Davin Dekker standing directly before them. No. His advance would be more insidious.

She checked for traffic, then tugged on Max's leash to force him across the street with her to St. Joe's. She concentrated on the way she moved, making her movements slow, normal, as she fastened his leash to the bike rack outside the gymnasium door. As she entered she left the door open so she could see—or at least hear—him when she went inside.

The large room went silent as the people gathered around the table at the opposite side of the room looked at her.

She held her breath. She'd completely forgotten that she was still little more than a stranger among these people she'd known all her life. That the last meeting had been her first and that they might not have expected her return. Or that with all that was going on in her life, the last place they expected to see her was there, casually taking part in arranging a holiday celebration.

Perhaps she'd been wrong to come here. Maybe she should have gone straight home. Or stopped by Mrs. O'Malley's to see if Mavis was still there.

Or tried to find Aidan.

A chair leg screeched against the polished wood floor, and suddenly everyone gathered at the table seemed to get up as one to approach her. Women hugged her, men greeted her, they all asked about Mavis's condition, they all asked about Aidan. But foremost, they made her feel connected to each and every one of them in a way she'd never expected or experienced before. They included her as part of the community she'd voluntarily spent a lifetime on the fringes of.

Mrs. Noonan loosely took her arm and led her toward the table. "We were all so sorry to hear about Mavis, Penelope. We trust she's going to be all right?"

"Define 'all right.'"

Mrs. Noonan gave her a surprised look, then laughed. "I'll take that as a yes."

Penelope nodded. "Yes, she's going to be all right."

"Have they caught the man who did it?" someone else asked.

Penelope shook her head as she took the seat they'd kept open, only afterward realizing that it was the one Aidan had sat in at the previous meeting. "No, they haven't. So I think everyone should be a little extra careful until they do."

Elva snorted from the far end of the table where she'd stayed put since Penelope entered the gymnasium. "I say Aidan Kendall is the only stranger in this town."

The room fell dead silent.

Penelope quietly cleared her throat. "Mr. Kendall was not involved in the attack, Elva."

"How could you know that?" the crotchety woman demanded.

Penelope lifted her chin. "Because he and I were together at the time of the break-in."

"Together as in..." someone else led.

Penelope felt her face burn. "Together as in none-of-your-business together."

Again, silence.

Penelope wondered if they would notice if she crawled under the table and stayed there for the remainder of the meeting.

"Go, Penelope," Jeanette said, punching the air with her fist.

Penelope giggled. Something she'd never done until Aidan had touched her and transformed her life and her outlook.

Avoiding everyone's gazes, she shuffled through the notes she'd brought along with her from the last meeting. Only after she'd read the last one did she realize that no one was saying anything.

She looked up to find them all staring at her.

It took her a minute to realize that they weren't focusing on her because her hair was messed up, or because she had a ginseng tea mustache or because they wanted detailed information on exactly what she and Aidan had been doing together last night. Rather, they expected her to lead the meeting.

"Oh," she whispered.

Then, with a quiet clearing of her throat, she did just that.

An hour and a half later, the last of the plans had been sewn up. Each of them had volunteered and been assigned a job to do tomorrow, to decorate Lucas Circle and get the play list to the high school band, and Penelope felt a hollow sense of satisfaction. During the entire ninety minutes her attention had constantly drifted to the open door, and Max had been sitting just beyond, on alert, his gaze fixed on something outside her line of vision. And with every sweep of the second hand on her watch, she was acutely aware that Aidan was out there somewhere, alone.

Quiet conversation between the members ensued, making Penelope feel as if she'd stepped into a bizarre scene from the play *A Midsummer Night's Dream*. Everything appeared so normal, mundane, when to her and Aidan things were anything but.

She was stacking her notes neatly, not looking forward to the walk home, when a thought occurred to her. She looked around the table from one to another of her fellow board members...no, her neighbors, and quietly cleared her throat. One by one they turned their attention to her.

"I want to ask a favor of you all," she began. And she made her first plea ever for help from people outside her immediate family.

Aidan sat in his car parked in the back corner of Dunwoody's Used Cars lot, which had closed at five, his gaze focused unwaveringly on the door to St. Joe's gymnasium. The skin of his neck prickled, as it had for the past hour and half when he'd followed Penelope there. He knew Davin was nearby. Knew it with everything in him.

What he had yet to ascertain was whether his twin was following him or Penelope.

Max's barking jerked his gaze to the large canine that had sat at attention since the moment Penelope had gone inside the gymnasium. He'd never known the dog to bark. Not once. He watched as Penelope came outside with the rest of the group, each of them seeming to linger by her side before drifting off to go home.

"Ask someone for a ride, Penelope," he whispered.

He glanced at the plum-colored sky on the western horizon where the sun had disappeared behind a bank of low-lying clouds. He didn't like the thought of her walking on the unpaved shoulder all alone in the dark, especially under the circumstances. Because if something were to happen to her...

She smiled and nodded at Mrs. Noonan, then followed the older woman to her car, Maximus in tow.

Aidan closed his eyes and let out a deep sigh of relief. Thank God.

All day he'd checked the local hotels and motels, asking personnel if he looked familiar to them, all the time avoiding detection from the law. There hadn't been a single sign of recognition anywhere he went. Was Davin traveling with someone? He found the possibility unlikely. Davin had been consumed for so long with evening some fictional score between them that he'd never really lived his own life. He lived only to make his twin's life a living hell.

And he'd succeeded admirably.

Aidan cursed under his breath. "Not anymore, little brother. Not anymore. You and me, we're going to have this out, once and for all."

What remained was where and when. And the question of whether he'd be the one to determine that or if Davin would. Allowing, of course, that Sheriff Parker didn't catch up with him first.

He watched as Mrs. Noonan drove out of St. Joe's parking lot, Penelope seated in front, Max in the back. Once they were out of sight, he reached down and switched on the ignition, then turned in the opposite direction, away from St. Joe's…and Penelope's house.

Penelope had Mrs. Noonan leave her off at the old bridge spanning the Old Valley River, explaining that she wanted to exercise Max a bit before they got home or else he would keep her and Mavis up all night with ceaseless barking. An untruth to be sure, but she wanted these few moments to herself on the bridge before she went home to an empty house. Or worse, to a house that held an ever-changing Mavis.

She waved as Mrs. Noonan made a U-turn and headed back to town. Then she crossed to the middle of the wood bridge, Max's nails clicking against the surface as he walked next to her, still on alert.

The sky was just light enough to reflect off the gurgling water disappearing under the bridge and coming out over an outcropping of rocks on the other side. She gripped the hand railing and leaned heavily against it, taking a deep breath of the cool air, the lush vegetation and everything that was reassuringly familiar to her.

Max barked and strained against his leash, nearly pulling it from her hand. She tightened her grip and quietly shushed him. She just needed this one moment to gather her wits—

"I've been waiting all day for an opportunity to see you again."

Penelope started, putting her free hand over her heart as she turned toward the sound of the voice she would recognize anywhere.

"Aidan!" she breathed. He stood a couple of feet away, his hands in the pockets of his Dockers, his grin making her flush from head to foot. Then she rushed to embrace him. She'd been so afraid she wouldn't see him again. So concerned that he would disappear and she would never know what had happened.

Suddenly she remembered where they were and the danger of his being spotted. She pulled away.

"Someone might see you."

He shook his head. "No. I made sure I wasn't followed."

She smiled. "Good."

Max tugged on the leash she held, backing away from Aidan. She briefly considered the dog's strange behavior, then stumbled back to Aidan. She turned toward the water, remembering the first time they'd met here. The first of many meetings that had turned her inside out and transformed her into a woman she no longer recognized in the mirror. The old Penelope had appeared older than her years, with pale skin, empty eyes and single-minded determination to make it through the day.

Now…

Now her hair seemed to shine more, her eyes were alive with love, and every moment of her day was filled with yearning for the man next to her, making her forget the time or what she should be doing...

Max continued to strain against his leash, his barking dropping off to a low growl.

Penelope frowned. "Max!" She said to Aidan, "I don't know what's gotten into him. He's been acting strange all night."

Aidan grinned. "That's all right. Hey, boy, don't you remember me?"

Max snapped at Aidan, and he took a small leap back.

"Whoa. I'd like to keep the hand if it's all the same to you."

Penelope suddenly felt a twinge of uneasiness.

"So, how did the meeting go tonight?" he asked.

Tension seeped from her muscles. Only Aidan would know about the meeting. Unless...

She shoved the thought from her mind.

"It went well, actually. Everything's done but, well, the doing."

"And your grandmother?"

"Fine. She's fine." She gestured in the direction of the house, still a half mile or so down the road. "I expect she's home now. That's why I stopped here. You know, to grab a few minutes to myself before walking the rest of the way." If she found it funny that before her life had been crammed with just such spare minutes, she wasn't going to admit it. She was so glad to see that Aidan was doing well. And that he had obviously missed her as much as she'd missed him…if he'd risked capture to see her.

She looked at the road behind him. "Where's your car?"

"My what?" He was staring at her face. "Oh. I parked it down the road a ways in an abandoned drive."

She nodded.

"I was just thinking how beautiful you are."

No matter how many times he told her that, she didn't think she would ever get used to it.

"May I kiss you?"

He'd never asked for permission before. He'd always just kissed her. Almost as if he were fighting an inner battle. On one side was the desire to touch her, on the other the need to lock her out. To keep himself and her safe.

She smiled, feeling awkward. "I'd love it if you'd kiss me."

He took his hands out of his pockets and stepped closer. Max bared his teeth.

Penelope gasped. "Max!" She yanked the leash hard. "Bad boy!" She pulled him back and fastened his lead to a support beam a couple of feet behind her. He barked in protest and she patted his head. "Easy, Maximus. It's okay. It's just Aidan."

Penelope turned to find him standing directly behind her, startling her for a second time.

He quirked a brow.

"I'm sorry. With everything going on, I guess I'm jumpy."

"Understandable."

He dropped his hands onto her shoulders and tugged her forward, nearly causing her to lose her balance. She laughed nervously. "Wow. I guess you *have* missed me."

"You have no idea…"

He dropped his head and pressed his lips to hers.

And Penelope's heart stopped beating in her chest. Because in that instant she knew that it wasn't Aidan she was kissing.

Chapter Sixteen

Aidan had never done anything more difficult in his life than watch Davin lean in to kiss Penelope. A sense of betrayal and acidy loathing coated his insides. The only saving grace was that he knew the exact moment when Penelope realized that the man she was kissing wasn't him, but Davin. He watched as her fingers curled into fists and the way her spine snapped upright.

He cursed, wishing he could have given her some sort of warning. But by the time he'd driven up near the bridge, Penelope had had her back to him and was tying Max to a beam, out of striking distance—when what she should have done was set the dog free to attack Davin.

Aidan reached for the door handle, but froze when Davin appeared satisfied with the success of his bold move and drew away from Penelope, leaving her staring, puzzled, up at him.

A mix of powerful emotions assaulted Aidan, freezing his hands to the steering wheel. At the first sight of his brother in fourteen months, snapshots from his life clicked through his mind. He and Davin as kids, breaking the windows of an abandoned house with stones, each throw a competition that Aidan always won. Him holding his sobbing, broken brother as their house burned to the ground, their parents still inside. Blurred shots of his wife smiling, then crying as she shared the devastating news that the baby she carried was not his, but his brother's. Roses pelting his wife's casket along with the steady rain…

And now, the image of Davin once again pretending to be him and making a move on Penelope.

Enraged, Aidan had to yank on the door handle several times before it finally gave, the jerky movement nearly spitting him out onto the pavement. He struggled to regain his balance as he ran for the bridge, his vision filled with the present and the past and his brain unable to register that Penelope was untying Maximus and waving goodbye to his brother. All he could think of was how much he wanted to kill the man who had stolen so much from him.

The thought should have caught him up short, should have made him think that perhaps contacting the authorities might be the better move. But with his heart thudding angrily against his rib cage, all he could think about was exacting his own type of revenge against the man who looked so much like him, but was nothing like him. His brother, his blood, his enemy.

He heard a roar, but didn't immediately identify it as coming from his own throat until he slammed against Davin's back, the move knocking them both to the wood planks of the bridge.

"Aidan!" He heard Penelope's gasp from somewhere beyond the white fog that crowded his head.

"Go! Get out of here, Penelope!" he shouted, hauling a fist back and burying it in his twin's face. "Call the sheriff's office. Now!"

Aidan's arm hovered in the air, ready to come down again. Davin's unconcerned expression as he stared up at him made his stomach turn. No emotion lurked there in those brown eyes. No guilt for having done what he had. No remorse for wreaking such havoc. Not even hate. Merely indifference.

His brother took advantage of his momentary distracted state and rolled him over until Aidan's back was against the wood and Davin was on top of him.

"Ah, you always were so predictable, weren't

you, big brother. I knew messing with your woman would bring you out of the bushes.''

This had all been some sort of ruse? Some dark plan designed to get him to tip his hand? Aidan's head swam with the information.

"You always did think you were the better one, Allen,'' Davin said. ''It's time to prove once and for all who is the smarter brother.''

Stars danced behind Aidan's eyes as Davin's fist connected with his brow. He struggled to push his brother off but only succeeded in further trapping himself. Suddenly, the weight on him disappeared. He blinked against a trickle of blood running from his brow into his eye, and found Davin standing over him, grinning in a malevolent way that made Aidan's blood run cold.

"It's said that the meek inherit the earth,'' Davin said, kicking his legs where he tried to get up. ''I say the meek are eaten by the strong, and it's the strong that inherit the earth.''

Somewhere in the back of his mind he registered that Penelope hadn't left. Instead she stood on the bridge, her face a model of horror, Max still tied to the support beam. He tried to tell her to leave, but a kick to his stomach left him without air.

"You never did figure it out, did you,'' Davin said, a spiteful grin making him look so different from Aidan that Aidan nearly didn't recognize him. ''That I was the one who set fire to our house.''

Aidan thought he might be sick. Fire…house? Was he referring to the fire that had taken their parents' lives?

He closed his eyes and memories crashed back on him like a wave of blinding color. He remembered waking up in the middle of the night to the acrid smell of smoke. Panicked, he'd felt around their shared bedroom for his brother. Davin hadn't been there. Coughing, he had crawled out into the hall to find flames licking up the side of the hall walls. He'd quickly backtracked into the bedroom and closed the door, using the wadded sheet he'd placed over his nose and mouth to block the smoke from getting in from the bottom of the door. Then he'd rushed for the window, all the time calling for his brother and his parents.

He remembered being relieved when he found Davin outside on the lawn, staring up in horror at the sight of their family home burning down.

Had it been horror? Or had it been sheer awe?

Aidan rose onto his elbows with some effort, taking shallow breaths that seemed to dredge up the taste of smoke and trying to force deeper ones. "Why?"

Davin shrugged as if they were discussing which college to attend or which restaurant to eat at, rather than the pointless loss of their parents.

"Why do you think? Because they had never really been my parents. They had always been yours." Davin drew a hand across his own mouth, coming away with blood. "Because they always chose you over me. For as long as I can remember, I thought about what it would be like to be an only child. But I knew that doing away with you, alone, wouldn't have done the trick. They would have mourned you and forgotten about me. So I decided to do away with you all and start again from scratch. With a family that would love me, and only me. Never compare me to a brother that was always one step ahead."

It didn't make any sense. Davin had killed their parents? It wasn't possible. Aidan remembered his twin being broken up, almost destroyed by the news.

Or had he been sorry that he, Allen, hadn't died along with their parents as planned?

The idea blindsided him. So much hate...

He watched as Penelope crept up behind Davin, something long and hard in her hand. A branch. Aidan fought harder to get up as he watched Penelope swing. Davin easily warded off the blow, then grabbed Penelope's silken black hair, filling his fist with the tresses.

Davin chuckled, pleased with himself. "My only regret is that I didn't kill beautiful Kathleen while you watched. But that's easily remedied, isn't it."

He pushed Penelope toward the opposite side of the bridge where large, jagged rocks broke the surface of the river.

Where Penelope's mother had taken her own life twenty years before.

"No!" Aidan shouted, as Davin pushed her over the railing.

One minute Penelope had been about to save Aidan by hitting Davin in the back of the head with a branch she'd scavenged from the other side of the bridge; the next she was sailing through the air, everything appearing to move in slow motion. She took in Davin's manic expression of satisfaction as he faced his brother. Saw Aidan's horror as he scrambled to his feet. Felt the cool air that hovered above the river seep in to saturate her very bones. A millisecond before her body would have made contact with the rocks that had taken her mother's life so long ago, she reached out, wildly clawing for a handhold—something, anything, that would prevent her fall. She found it, latching with barely the tips of her fingers onto the wooden slats of the bridge, the sudden action nearly dislocating her right shoulder. But there she hung on for dear life.

"What's the execution method Ohio employs?" She heard Davin's voice as she pulled herself up so that her forearms rested against the wood and she could see the two men. "Death by electrocution? Fortuitous, don't you think, that you chose to come here. Rhode Island's method of lethal injection is far too humane. I want you to fry. And I want it to happen knowing that you're being punished not only for Kathleen's death, but for Penelope Moon's.''

Penelope's arms ached and pulled from where she hung on to the narrow ledge. She slipped slightly, and looked down at where the rocks waited for her. Her throat choked off all air as she remembered the pictures of her mother's battered body that the local newspaper had run on the front page. *Fate runs in a circle,* she remembered her grandmother telling her once. Although she'd been ten at the time and heartbroken by the ruthless teasing she'd suffered at school that day, Penelope applied the saying to the here and now.

Was this her fate? To die in the same way her mother had?

She must have made a sound when she nearly lost her grip, because she looked up to find Davin grinning at her with evil intent. She heard a shout behind him.

''No!''

She watched as Davin lurched forward against the railing. Had Aidan hit him from behind? The sudden move shook the bridge enough to make her grip more precarious. She was fighting to get a better hold when one of Davin's feet prodded at her fingers.

Oh, God, she was going to fall.

Then he was gone from sight.

Penelope held on, but the muscles of her fingers and arms were under tremendous strain, and they felt on the verge of giving out. She heard a *crack* and peered through the railing slats to watch Aidan repeatedly punch his brother. Then Davin roared and pinned him against the opposite side of the bridge. On they battled, first one, then the other gaining the upper hand as Penelope fought to maintain her hold, seeking a foothold and finding nothing but cold, empty air.

Max's incessant barking drew her attention, and she found his eyes moving from the fighting men to her and back again, straining until his chain collar bit into his neck. Penelope's eyes burned with tears at his futile attempt to help her.

If only she had heeded his warnings. If only she had untied him. If only she had let Mrs. Noonan drive her all the way home instead of dropping her off at the bridge.

She jerked her attention back to the two men, finding it amazingly easy to tell them apart, now that they were together. Davin's face was drawn in sharp, pale lines, his jaw tight, his mouth a gash against his skin, his brow lowered and dark.

And Aidan…

Her heart surged into her throat as he took a blow to his already bleeding brow and sagged against the opposite railing. Then she watched Davin cross to pick up the branch that she had intended to use on him. The irony that Aidan would be hit with the branch she had chosen to try to save him with made her dizzy with the unfairness of it all.

"Aidan!" she cried, slipping another inch.

His eyes snapped open and focused on her, then on the wood swinging for his head. He ducked and caught his brother around the waist, pushing him until he was against the other railing, mere feet from where Penelope hung on. The wood flew from Davin's grip and sailed over the railing, wedging between the rocks like a deadly spear just under Penelope's dangling feet.

She slipped again and screamed.

"Aidan, please!" she yelled, knowing even as she did so that it was unfair to ask him to save her when he was trying so hard to save himself.

Her right hand slid completely off the ledge, leaving her left arm trembling with the strain it took to hold her weight.

Then her fingers started to give way. She summoned every ounce of strength she had to maintain her grip, but couldn't do it. She watched in terror as her fingers slid completely free...and she was airborne—

Aidan's hand clamped tightly around her wrist, stopping her descent. She looked up to find his face straining with the effort it took to keep her from falling. But more than that, she saw relief and love.

She looked down to find Davin skewered by the tree branch, his unmoving body bobbing in the churning water around the rocks.

* * *

Hours later Penelope huddled on the west bank of the river, wishing there was a way she could avoid ever going over the bridge again. The wool blanket the sheriff had draped over her shoulders was doing little to chase away the chill that permeated every cell of her body. Sheriff's deputies milled around, the lights on the top of the squad cars filling the night with an eerie red and blue glow. A spotlight revealed the body lying on top of the rocks.

Penelope shuddered and turned away—the man looked so much like Aidan...

She noticed the sheriff grilling Aidan where he sat in the back of a squad car, his arms handcuffed behind his back. Even with the proof that Aidan had a twin, and with Penelope's corroboration, the sheriff appeared reluctant to buy their story.

Half of Old Orchard had come out to ogle from the other side of the yellow crime-scene tape stretched across the opposite end of the bridge. A collective gasp went up as the spotlight illuminated the body; then, after a heartbeat of silence, the chatter level rose as they all openly speculated about what happened.

Penelope heard someone raise her voice, and the crowd reluctantly parted. Mavis popped out, Mrs. O'Malley on her heels. Relief rushed through Penelope, but her body seemed incapable of following her command to stand.

"Let me through, you imbecile. That's my granddaughter over there." Mavis swatted at the arm of a young deputy who was trying to keep her from ducking under the tape.

The deputy seemed taken aback by a particularly strong whack and let her under.

"Me, um, too," Mrs. O'Malley said, shadowing Mavis's heels.

"What happened?" Mavis asked, crouching down before Penelope and smoothing the hair from her face.

Penelope hadn't realized her teeth were chattering until that moment. She tried for a smile and said, "You remember that life you said we both needed to lead? Well, I'd say I've now officially had enough excitement to last for the next two incarnations."

"Oh, baby," Mavis said, enveloping Penelope in her arms. Max nudged his nose between them, seemingly in need of some loving care himself.

"What's going on here?" Penelope heard Mrs. O'Malley say to someone. Penelope realized she was addressing the sheriff. She pointed her finger in a way that Penelope had seen her do countless times when she was a kid and Mrs. O'Malley was a high school teacher who could calm the rowdiest of classrooms.

"You take those handcuffs off Aidan this instant, Mr. Parker. This instant, do you hear me?" She pointed to the side of the bridge. "It doesn't take a rocket scientist to figure out that Aidan is innocent. I always suspected you were a little on the slow side, boy. Don't prove me right.''

Penelope watched as Sheriff Parker pushed his hat back on his head. "It's Sheriff now, Mrs. O. And you shouldn't be here."

"I don't care what you call yourself now, Mr. Parker. That man is innocent and you're making yourself look like a fool."

Mavis raised a brow at Penelope. Penelope stared back at her, just now realizing she wore makeup. And her hair looked as if it had just come out of curlers. She glanced at Mrs. O'Malley and found the same thing.

Strange...

"I have to agree with Mrs. O'Malley, here," Mayor Nelson said as he ducked under the crime tape, tugging on the lapels of his ever-present suit jacket and walking across the bridge. "Release that man at once, Sheriff Parker."

Of course, everyone knew the history between the two men. Mayor Nelson's nephew Blakely "Bully" Wentworth had lost to Cole Parker in the last sheriff's election.

The sheriff hiked his pants up higher on his slender hips. "Can't do that, Mayor. Not until I clear up everything."

"You can clear it up later," Mrs. O'Malley said. "Aidan's not going anywhere anytime soon. Are you, son?"

Penelope looked hopefully at Aidan. He met her gaze, then quickly averted his eyes.

"No, ma'am."

He was lying. Penelope wasn't sure how she knew it, but he planned to leave Old Orchard—and her—behind.

The sheriff faced Aidan and heaved a heavy sigh. "Fine. Get up so I can take the handcuffs off."

The crowd on the other side of the bridge cheered, but Penelope felt a leaden weight drop into the middle of her stomach.

Despite everything that had happened, or maybe because of it, Aidan was going to leave.

Chapter Seventeen

The next morning Penelope started her day just as she started every day. Only, this morning her muscles ached and her heart thudded dully. Not even her grandmother's having put the doors back on, having taken down all the pictures of her mother, or the fact that Mavis was out back mixing plaster following the directions on the back of a store-bought package, could make her feel any better.

I've got to go, Penelope, Aidan had said to her last night after the sheriff let him walk her home.

Mavis and Mrs. O'Malley had started to follow, but seemed to think better of it. Instead they had

lingered with the townsfolk, presumably to give
Penelope and Aidan some time alone.

"But you told the sheriff..." Her voice had
drifted off. "There's no reason for you to leave,
Aidan. Not anymore."

He'd smiled at her sadly and kissed her on the
nose. "There's a very good reason why I have to
leave."

Then he'd kissed her until her knees gave out
and walked into the night without a backward
glance.

His leaving didn't make any sense—now that
everything else seemed to be falling into place....

"The mayor asked me out on a date," the old
woman said.

Penelope absently spread low-cal cream cheese
on a bagel, barely noticing that Max was licking it
as she spread. She shooed him away, then stared
at Mavis standing in the doorway with what looked
like a metal spatula on steroids, filled with what
she guessed was plaster. There was another smaller
metal spatula in the other hand.

"What?"

"I said, the mayor asked me on a date." She
strode by Penelope and walked into the other room.

Penelope fed Max her breakfast and followed
her grandmother. She caught up with her in the
dining room, where she'd already filled half the
holes she'd made.

Mavis shrugged. "Well, to be honest, it's not a

date date, but he did ask Edith and me to join him at his table at tomorrow's festivities.''

"That doesn't qualify as a date, Gram.''

Mavis focused her unsettling dark eyes on her. "At my age, a shared smile is a torrid affair, Popi.''

Penelope shook her head and looked at her watch. "I've got to go. I'll be at the shop for an hour or so. Then I'll be joining everyone in the square to get ready for tomorrow and the Fourth of July celebration. Are you still going to meet me there?''

"Edith and I wouldn't miss it.''

Penelope made a face. It seemed every few words out of her grandmother's mouth were "Edith and I'' this and "Edith and I'' that.

"Fine.''

She snapped on Max's leash, wondering how she could get across the river without going over the bridge.

The memory of the pain in Penelope's dark eyes haunted Aidan throughout the night as he drove toward a destination he feared he would never reach. He didn't know why he hadn't been able to tell her where he was going, and why it was so important that he go there, immediately. Maybe it was because of his own uncertainty. Or the guilt.

So much guilt...

As he ran his hand over his face, the sunrise

popped over the horizon in his rearview mirror and the highway sign before him read Sullivan, Missouri. He'd been on the road for eight hours straight, and aside from stopping for gas and to fill up on caffeine, he'd driven straight through. Past semi trucks out on their weekly runs. Past the kind of highway patrol cars that had inspired fear in him before last night. Pushing himself toward this one last door from his past that had been left ajar.

Within a half hour he was parked on a quiet residential street not unlike the streets of Old Orchard. A couple of houses away a woman worked in her garden. Farther on, a boy was tossing papers onto porches from his bike. Aidan heard the distant whine of a lawn mower even this early on the day before the official holiday.

His gaze fastened on the simple, one-story house whose address he had memorized but not written down for fear Davin would get his hands on the information. Inside was a distant cousin of Brody Tanner's…and four-year-old Joshua.

The front door to the house opened and a young blond woman wearing a pink satin robe picked up the paper, then went back inside. Aidan's heartbeat thundered in his ears. He should have called Brody and had him contact his cousin's family to let them know he was coming. He should have given them warning. But he hadn't expected the need to see the boy to hit him so powerfully when everything came to a head last night.

Would Joshua recognize him? What had he been told about the father who had been accused of his mother's murder? Was he old enough to understand? Would Joshua want to see him? Or would Aidan be upsetting a carefree life that was much better without him?

His fingers tightened on the steering wheel. Maybe it had been a mistake to come—

The screen door slapped against its frame, and Aidan glanced up to find the woman standing in the doorway again…looking after a young boy who was darting out into the front yard with an older boy, both of them wearing ball mitts.

Oh, God, he's grown so much.

And he was the spitting image of Kathleen.

Aidan blindly reached for the door handle and let himself out of the car before he even realized he was going to do so, his gaze glued to the young figure lobbing a ball at the older boy. He met the young woman's gaze through the screen door. She stiffened. He held up his hands, and all at once she seemed to realize who he was. She nodded her approval and hugged herself.

Aidan's knees seemed to weaken the closer he drew to the yard and the boys. Would Joshua understand that Aidan had sent him away for his own protection? Not just from his uncle, but from having to witness the possible arrest of his father? Would he see that what he'd done had been done out of love and a desire to see Joshua have a safe, stable family to love him?

Would he recognize Aidan at all?

"Joshua." He murmured the boy's name as the woman opened the screen door and called for the other child, likely her son.

The towheaded younger boy watched his friend walk toward the house, puzzled, holding the ball tightly in his glove. Then he slowly turned toward Aidan's voice.

Aidan knew a moment of love, of fear, so great he nearly collapsed with the power of it.

He doesn't recognize me....

He tried to reason it out. The lack of reaction was only natural. He hadn't seen the boy for over a year. And Joshua had been only three then, barely aware of himself as a person, much less of anyone else.

But the reality cut Aidan to the bone, creating in him a pain so deep, so acute that—

"Dad?"

At the sound of that one word, so simple really, Aidan's legs threatened to give out on him. He dropped to his knees and held his arms out. "Joshua."

Joshua dropped the ball and mitt and slammed his young body against Aidan's. Aidan enfolded him in his arms, holding him so tightly he was sure the poor kid couldn't breathe.

This little human being who looked so much like Kathleen was his blood, his kin, the only family he had left in the world.

His son...

Chapter Eighteen

Fourth of July

Penelope lingered on the fringe of the group of townspeople crowded into Lucas Circle. All around her people were busy playing carnival games, drinking free punch, listening to the sound of a local jazz band that had replaced the high school band two hours earlier. The sun had just set and soon it would be time for the fireworks display to begin in Old Man McCreary's farm, just over the south skyline. Nearby, Mavis and Edith O'Malley sat on either side of the mayor, vying for his attention and getting it in spades, making the older man grin as if he'd been given his Christmas present early.

But despite the festive atmosphere that she had helped create, Penelope felt as hollow as the papier-mâché sculpture of Uncle Sam that someone had erected near the fountain. She listlessly walked through the area where families were spreading blankets on the lush grass near the fountain or setting up chairs in the surrounding streets that had been closed off to traffic, kids of all ages tracing their names with glowing sparklers. She absently sat down on the concrete lip of the wall surrounding the fountain and looked up at the man-made stars in the trees above her, then at the real things in the sky above.

She sighed wistfully. The busyness of the past two days ebbed away, leaving a void that held nothing but Aidan's name.

Where was he? she wondered. Was he thinking of her, just as she was sitting there thinking of him?

"Great job on the decorations, Penelope," Darby Parker Conrad Sparks said, passing by with her husband, John, her twin seven-year-old girls and a baby stroller.

Penelope weakly smiled her thanks, trying not to stare at the twins, who were arguing over a lollipop.

She wondered at the tremendous change her life had undergone in the past couple weeks. Where

just last year—and every year before that—she and
Mavis had barely recognized the holiday, much
less celebrated it, now both of them were participating in the public celebration. Where they once
might have caught a glimpse of the tops of the
fireworks over the forest bordering their land, now
they had the best seats in the house.

And she would trade it all for just five more
minutes alone with Aidan.

She missed him so much sometimes that she
feared her heart might collapse in on itself. This
from a woman who had learned to rely only on
herself for so many years. No friends. No family
beyond her occasionally crazy grandmother. Only
her shop and her dog, and the sporadic presence
of the town cat.

Now…

Well, now that she knew there was oh-so-much
more to life, now that she'd been touched by love's
magic brush, she longed to have everything.

She'd never really seen herself as a mother.
Never imagined herself a wife. Never considered
living in a house that was truly hers.

She thought about her brush with death, hanging
over the same rocks that had taken her mother's
life—and she shivered. The temperature was warm
but still she wrapped her arms around herself to
ward off a chill. What had it been like for her
mother, standing there staring at those rocks and
thinking that there was nothing to live for? Not her

mother, not even her young daughter? What had it taken to make her climb over that ledge and jump? And what had she thought of in those last moments before death took her? Had she even considered the solemn map that she was charting for her family? Had she regretted her action two seconds too late? Or had her last thought been of the man who had come to town? Penelope's unnamed father who had swept Heather Moon off her feet, then left her, pregnant and alone, to face the future?

Penelope looked down to find herself caressing her flat stomach. What she wouldn't give to be pregnant with Aidan's baby. To have something that was so solidly, undeniably his. A breathing reminder of the precious moments they had shared—

''Penelope?''

She looked up, a light sheen of tears blurring her vision. She had to have imagined Aidan's voice. He'd left her two days ago with no promise to return. She blinked against the moisture that obscured the figure standing some ten feet away. Her heart skipped a beat. No, not one figure. Two.

She wiped at the dampness on her cheeks. Her gaze dropped to the face of a boy of no more than four or five, with hair the color of corn at the peak of ripeness, looking at her with the biggest blue eyes she'd ever seen. She jerked her eyes upward to stare into Aidan's face, understanding in that one moment why he'd had to leave her with no promise for tomorrow. He'd still had commitments that stretched to yesterday.

She unsteadily rose to her feet as Aidan moved closer. His large hand was wrapped around the much smaller one, the boy moving easily, trustingly, with his father.

"Hi," she said, unsure as she stared into Aidan's hopeful, loving eyes. She swallowed the emotion blocking her throat, then crouched down. "And who do we have here?"

The boy shyly looked down, then back up. "My name's Joshua Burford...I mean Dekker."

Penelope's smile was quick and all-encompassing. She slowly extended her hand, watching in wonder and fascination as the young boy took it. "Well, hello, Joshua Burford Dekker. I'm Penelope Moon." So small, so delicate, so sweet. "It's very nice to meet you."

Something on his wrist caught her eye. She recognized the leather strap wrapped around his hand twice, the Greek eye twinkling under the white lights strung from the trees. She glanced up at Aidan to find such a look of pride and love on his face that it took her breath away.

She reluctantly released her grip. She wanted to keep the small hand in hers forever.

"My daddy says you're going to be my new mommy."

"What?" she whispered, looking from the boy's hopeful face to Aidan's.

Aidan chuckled softly. "I said I'd like it if Penelope would consider the position."

The boy tilted his head slightly, staring up at her. Then he nodded. "I'd like it, too."

Overwhelmed with happiness. Joy. Love. That's how Penelope felt as Aidan looked at her.

"So what do you say, Penelope? Would you like to become a member of the ragtag Dekker clan?"

He held out a ring box.

Max chose that moment to remind them of his presence, sticking his nose between them and sniffing at something on the front of Joshua's shirt.

"Oh, cool, a dog!" The boy enthusiastically patted Max's head. "Is this Max?"

Neither Penelope nor Aidan answered him. They were too busy gazing at each other. Not that it mattered. It seemed Max had found his match in energy as he tackled the boy to the ground. Joshua laughed and hugged the dog's beefy neck, begging for mercy.

Penelope honestly didn't know what to say as the first of the fireworks shot up overhead. The townsfolk clapped their approval, as she and Aidan and Joshua and Max stood in the middle of them all, a part of them, yet separate. Alone, yet together. The town was a patchwork quilt woven of many colors and textures and styles.

And looking at Aidan, Penelope could see their square come together with delicate ease.

"Are you asking me to marry you, Aidan?" she whispered.

His half grin made her toes curl in her sandals. "That's usually what a ring like this means."

With a flick of his thumb he popped open the box. And there, nestled in black velvet, was a perfect oval sapphire in platinum.

He began to get down on one knee, and Penelope knew a moment of panic. She wanted to tell him to get up before anyone saw him.

Too late. She noticed that heads were beginning to turn away from the fireworks display and toward them.

"Penelope Moon, will you marry me? Will you promise to love me as I love you? Will you love and care for my son and pack our lunches and help me with school fund-raisers and zany town projects? Will you fill my heart with happiness and my bed with—"

Nearby, Mrs. O'Malley cleared her throat. Penelope noticed Joshua attached to Max's neck but watching, wide-eyed and eager.

"—flowers," Aidan finished, sliding Mrs. Noonan a sly glance.

Penelope laughed softly.

"Flowers? Why would anyone want flowers in their bed?" Joshua asked, his face creased in a comic grimace.

Penelope laughed again, unsure what to say, unsure if there really was anything she could say that would match the swell of emotion in her heart. But she was sure of one thing. That she and Aidan were meant to be together. And that the little boy next to them was a vital part of that love.

"Yes," she said simply. "Well, except for the making lunch part. You, um, may want to do that yourself."

Aidan rose and put the ring on her finger. Penelope marveled at it against her pale skin, then at him as he enveloped her in a hug. Max barked, and Joshua wound his skinny arms around them both, holding tight. The fireworks exploded, but there was a healthy round of clapping and hooting and whistling from spectators more interested in the couple near the fountain.

Penelope hugged the two men who would be a part of her life. The one man she had grown to love, the other she had fallen in love with on sight. She caught a movement out of the corner of her eye and shifted her gaze to watch Spot twitch her tail, apparently in approval, then turn and disappear into the night.

Epilogue

Six months later

Maybe having Christmas dinner at the house hadn't been such a great idea. A strand of hair hung over Penelope's face as she stuck her gloved hand inside the turkey, grabbing out the gizzard, heart, liver and neck that the recipe card on the counter told her she needed to make the dressing. She moved to push her hair out of the way but found both gloved hands covered with gunk. She settled instead for blowing the strand out of the way, only to watch as it drifted down again, impeding her vision.

She'd never cooked a turkey in her life. And she was beginning to wonder if now was the time to start.

She eyed the bottle of cooking sherry on the counter and considered opening it, even though it was only eleven o'clock in the morning.

Laughter drifted in from the living room, chasing the grimace from her face and replacing it with a blissful smile. Aidan and Joshua were playing with all the gifts Santa had left under their tree that morning.

In the past six months she and Aidan—he'd decided to keep the name, softly telling her that his real name was connected to too many bad memories while his life as Aidan was bonded to only good—had gotten married at the courthouse with far more than the handful of people she had expected to be present. They'd moved Aidan and Joshua into Mavis's old house, and, it seemed, within the blink of an eye the ramshackle structure had been transformed into something from a Norman Rockwell painting. When Aidan wasn't working at St. Joe's, he and Joshua were working on one of their many home projects. Everything had been painted, repaired, replaced and decorated. And while their house didn't exactly match up with other houses, with its purple painted shudders and yellow stars etched into the porch railing, it was home. Their home.

And Penelope was happier than she'd ever been. Or she would be if she could only get this blasted turkey in the oven so she could go join Aidan and Joshua in the fun.

"Do you need any help?"

Penelope glanced over her shoulder to find Aidan standing with his hands braced against the doorjamb, as if hesitant to come in. Not that she could blame him. She'd chased him from the kitchen no fewer than three times so far this morning.

She watched Joshua peek at her from behind Aidan's hip, then push through into the room. He linked his small arms around her legs.

"Can I help, Popi?"

She glanced down at the munchkin who had brought so much sunshine to her and Aidan's lives. Four-year-old Joshua was so generous and loving and such a happy boy despite all he'd gone through.

He was also a fellow Capricorn, which meant that she and he got along exceedingly well. And it also meant he had a birthday coming up, while hers had just passed.

She and Aidan had agreed that they should allow Joshua to decide if and when he would call her Mom. Which might be never, since he'd overheard Mavis call her Popi and had started calling her the pet name with great enthusiasm. But that was fine with Penelope. She was happy to include the little boy in her life, and she caught her breath when she saw the love in his deep blue eyes.

Penelope glanced at Joshua's father, the outnumbered Scorpio. She smiled secretly, wistfully. What would he say when he discovered he was to be outnumbered again by one? Not by another Capricorn, but rather, by a little Leo?

Shortly after they were married, he'd gone and had the necessary surgery to clear the block that would have prevented them from adding to their family. Both of them had been too busy to talk about the possibility of her being pregnant over the past two months, but she'd confirmed last week that she was carrying his child, purposely holding off until today to tell him.

There was a brief knock on the front door, and they heard Mavis call out, "Is it safe to come in?"

After Aidan's return to Old Orchard with little Joshua in tow, Mavis had decided that she liked staying with Edith O'Malley. Liked the action of the town. Liked that she didn't have to wait until summer to wreak havoc on her neighbors.

And, Penelope supposed, the move probably made it easier for her to date Mayor Nelson.

"Grammy!" Joshua called out, releasing Penelope's legs and throwing himself into Mavis's arms when Aidan moved to let her into the kitchen.

It never failed to touch Penelope to see how well the two got along. It seemed that Mavis filled some sort of void in Joshua's life, and he in return did the same for her.

"Merry Christmas," Aidan said, giving Mavis

a kiss on the cheek that made the old woman blush, then doing the same to Mrs. O'Malley, who as usual had come along.

"Careful or you'll make me drop the bird," Edith said, maneuvering around the logjam near the doorway.

Penelope blinked at her. "Bird?"

Mrs. O'Malley smiled at her, then took in the uncooked turkey on the counter. "First mistake all women make, sweetie. Tom should have been in the oven hours ago."

Penelope stared at the recipe card, then turned it over. Her shoulders slumped and she sighed in frustration and annoyance.

Mrs. O'Malley put a pan down on top of the stove, then draped an arm over her shoulders. "Don't worry about it. Stuff Tom in the fridge and I'll help you make him later."

Penelope smiled her thanks at the woman who had become like another grandmother to her.

"Humph."

Mavis's sound of disapproval pulled all gazes to where she stood in the middle of the kitchen, her too-thin arms crossed over her chest, staring at Penelope.

"What?" Penelope asked hesitantly, afraid of what her grandmother was up to now.

"Nothing. I'm just wondering when you planned to tell us all about what you already have cooking in your own little oven."

Penelope's mouth fell open. Her gaze flew to Aidan's shocked face. How was it possible that she knew?

Mrs. O'Malley patted Penelope on the shoulder where she still had her arm around her. "Don't worry. She doesn't have X-ray vision or supernatural powers. We ran into Bernice at the General Store yesterday morning. She's Dr. Tinsdale's nurse, you know. Anyway, she shared the good news."

Aidan slowly came to stand in front of Penelope, hope and love filling his rich brown eyes. "Is it true?"

"Is what true?" Joshua asked, pushing his way through the forest of adult legs so he could look up at Penelope.

She smiled down at him and rested her hand on his head. She looked back up at Aidan. "Yes," she breathed. "In eight short months the Dekker family is going to grow to include one more." Penelope crouched down so that she was eye level with Joshua. "And you're going to have a little brother or sister."

Joshua's features were sober as he considered her. Then he grinned and said, "Cool!"

Aidan helped Penelope back to her feet and embraced her so tightly she couldn't breathe. She laughed, returning the hug with equal intensity.

"Congratulations, Daddy. It looks like the operation was successful."

Aidan waggled his brows at her. "You have no idea...."

He kissed her, which shoved every thought from her mind. Vaguely she registered Joshua saying, "There they go again," then Mrs. O'Malley suggesting that maybe they should leave the two newlyweds alone. Then, as she heard footsteps leaving the kitchen, she heard Mavis retort, "Newlyweds? They're not newlyweds anymore. They're an old married couple with one kid already and another on the way."

Penelope smiled as she cuddled closer to Aidan. "I like the sound of that," she whispered to her husband.

He grinned back at her. "I do, too."

* * * * *

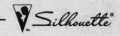

If you enjoyed what you just read,
then we've got an offer you can't resist!

Take 2 bestselling love stories FREE!

Plus get a FREE surprise gift!

Clip this page and mail it to Silhouette Reader Service™

IN U.S.A.	IN CANADA
3010 Walden Ave.	P.O. Box 609
P.O. Box 1867	Fort Erie, Ontario
Buffalo, N.Y. 14240-1867	L2A 5X3

YES! Please send me 2 free Silhouette Special Edition® novels and my free surprise gift. After receiving them, if I don't wish to receive anymore, I can return the shipping statement marked cancel. If I don't cancel, I will receive 6 brand-new novels every month, before they're available in stores! In the U.S.A., bill me at the bargain price of $3.99 plus 25¢ shipping and handling per book and applicable sales tax, if any*. In Canada, bill me at the bargain price of $4.74 plus 25¢ shipping and handling per book and applicable taxes**. That's the complete price and a savings of at least 10% off the cover prices—what a great deal! I understand that accepting the 2 free books and gift places me under no obligation ever to buy any books. I can always return a shipment and cancel at any time. Even if I never buy another book from Silhouette, the 2 free books and gift are mine to keep forever.

235 SDN DNUR
335 SDN DNUS

Name	(PLEASE PRINT)	
Address	Apt.#	
City	State/Prov.	Zip/Postal Code

* Terms and prices subject to change without notice. Sales tax applicable in N.Y.
** Canadian residents will be charged applicable provincial taxes and GST.
 All orders subject to approval. Offer limited to one per household and not valid to
 current Silhouette Special Edition® subscribers.
 ® are registered trademarks of Harlequin Books S.A., used under license.

SPED02   ©1998 Harlequin Enterprises Limited

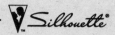

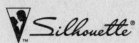

SPECIAL EDITION

#1603 PRICELESS—Sherryl Woods
Million Dollar Destinies
Famed playboy Mack Carlton loved living the fast life—with even faster women—until he met Dr. Beth Browning. Beth's reserved, quiet ways brought out the deepest emotions in Mack, and soon had him wanting to believe in a slow and easy, forever kind of love. Could Mack convince Beth that his bachelor days were over?

#1604 FOREVER...AGAIN—Maureen Child
Merlyn County Midwives
You don't get a second chance at forever. That's what widower Ron Bingham believed. But, then, he hadn't counted on meeting PR whiz Lily Cunningham. The carefree beauty brought laughter and passion back into his life and made him wonder—was love even sweeter the second time around?

#1605 CATTLEMAN'S HEART—Lois Faye Dyer
Chaotic. That was the only way Rebecca Wallingford could describe her latest business trip. The superorganized accountant had been sent to oversee the expansion of a certain Jackson Rand's ranch. She'd never meant to get pulled into a whirlwind love affair with the rugged rancher...and she certainly hadn't planned on liking it!

#1606 THE SHEIK & THE PRINCESS IN WAITING—
Susan Mallery
Prince Reyhan had been commanded by his father, the King of Bahania, to marry as befit his position. There was just one tiny matter in the way: divorcing his estranged wife, Emma Kennedy. Seeing sweet Emma again brought back a powerful attraction...and something deeper. Could Reyhan choose duty over his heart's desire?

#1607 THE BEST OF BOTH WORLDS—Elissa Ambrose
Single. Unemployed. Pregnant. Becky Roth had a lot on her mind...not to mention having to break her pregnancy news to the father, Carter Prescott III. They'd shared one amazing night of passion. But small-town, small-*time* Becky was no match for Carter's blue-blooded background. The fact that she was in love with him didn't change a thing.

#1608 IN HER HUSBAND'S IMAGE—Vivienne Wallington
Someone was trying to sabotage Rachel Hammond's ranch. The widowed single mom's brother-in-law, Zack Hammond, arrived and offered to help find the culprit...but the sexy, rugged photographer stirred up unwelcome memories of their scandalous past encounter. Now it was just a matter of time before a shattering secret was revealed!

SSECNM0304R